Secrets of the River

Janene Morgan

This is a work of fiction. Characters, institutions and organisations mentioned in this novel are either the product of the author's imagination or, if real, used fictitiously without any intent to describe actual conduct. The moral right of the author to be identified as the author of this work has been asserted.

Published by Reads on the Road

ISBN 978-1-7645341-2-3

Chapter One

No matter how often Maggie Ellis crossed the bridge to town, her eyes were drawn to the river below. Seven years of living here, and she never tired of its timeless beauty and power.

It ran alongside the road into town, wide and steady, the surface broken only by the occasional branch or leaf drifting past. She slowed as she crossed the bridge, her steps measured, her gaze dropping instinctively to the water below. It was higher than she remembered it the day before, after the overnight rain. Not alarmingly so, but enough to change how it moved. The current had more purpose, pulling a little harder at the edges. The clouds were still there, and the weather report indicated there was a good chance of more showers today.

She rested her hands on the railing for a moment, listening. The river always had a sound, although most people noticed only when it was in flood. Maggie heard it every day. Today it sounded fuller, as if it had something to say.

She straightened and continued on her way with her umbrella tucked under her arm, just in case the weather report was right for once.

Wattle River township, named for the river itself, was easing into the morning. Shopfronts opened one by one, keys rattling, doors swinging wide. A delivery truck idled outside the general store. Someone laughed further down the street. The air smelled faintly of damp earth and eucalyptus, lingering long after the rain had passed. The main street was wider than most, lined with an assortment of shops and shaded by trees planted decades earlier, providing relief during the long, dry summers.

Maggie liked this time of day best. The town felt quieter and more settled in the morning, before it properly woke. Not that Wattle River was a thriving hub of activity. Like many small country towns, it was a place where little happened on the surface, but beneath that calm lurked a long memory. If you looked closely enough, it held its share of secrets.

She walked with her bag tucked against her side, library keys familiar in her pocket. Maggie had lived here long enough that most people nodded or gave a friendly wave as she passed. Someone called her name from across the road, and she lifted a hand in return, smiling without breaking stride. In a small town, almost everyone knew everyone else. This was both a blessing and, at times, a curse.

At The Riverbend Café, Helen Carter was already inside, the lights glowing warmly through the front windows. Maggie watched her unlock the door and step in, efficient and unhurried. Helen had run the café as long as Maggie could remember, possibly longer. There were constants in town, and Helen was one of them. She kept the locals fuelled with caffeine and home-baked, country-style goodies, and knew the rhythms of Wattle River as well as anyone. People came and went, and Helen noticed. Bits of news travelled easily through the café, carried on coffee cups and casual conversation.

The bell chimed as Maggie pushed the door open, the welcome aroma of freshly brewed coffee wrapping around her like a familiar greeting. Buying coffee was something Maggie never questioned. She believed some things in life were necessities, and good coffee was one of them.

'Morning,' Helen said, looking up with a smile that reached her eyes.

'Morning,' Maggie replied as she set her bag down on the chair she always chose. 'Bit of a dreary morning.'

'Yes, it's still been a busy start, though.'

Helen turned back to the machine without asking what she wanted. Maggie watched her movements as she reached for the caramel syrup.

'Light milk, please,' Maggie said more out of habit than necessity.

Helen gave a small laugh. 'I know.'

The coffee arrived moments later, with smooth foam and the sweetness balanced just the way Maggie liked it. She wrapped her hands around the mug and took a careful sip. Perfect.

There were only a handful of people in the

café. Two men in work boots and hard hats sat near the window, speaking quietly over extra-large takeaway coffees. Mrs Kearney occupied her usual table in the corner, her handbag neatly placed at her feet and the newspaper folded on the table. Maggie noticed that she hadn't touched her coffee or the chocolate croissant on the plate beside it.

Helen leaned against the counter. 'River's up.'

'Yes,' Maggie replied. 'I noticed.'

Helen tilted her head slightly. 'Feels like it's been raining longer than forecast.'

Maggie nodded. Weather forecasts were little more than suggestions in Wattle River. The town was well acquainted with floods and droughts over the years, and like most country people, the locals took it in their stride, but the river was always a topic of conversation.

Maggie finished her coffee, thanked Helen, and stepped outside. The light had shifted while she'd been inside, brightening the street, glinting on windows and the river beyond. She crossed to the library at the end of the main street, facing the roundabout, and unlocked the door. The familiar click echoed softly in the quiet space.

The library smelled the way it always did. Paper, polish, something faintly dusty yet familiar. There was also a faint, lingering scent of fresh paint from the children's reading area, which had recently undergone a colourful makeover. Maggie turned on the lights, moved through the aisles, straightening chairs and reshelving a book someone had left in the wrong place. She liked beginning the day this way, alone with only the books and her thoughts.

At her desk, she set down her bag and

pulled out her notebook. Not the one she used for work, but the smaller one she kept for herself. She opened it, then closed it again without writing anything.

Maggie thought of Martin, likely already in his shed, the radio murmuring as he worked on whatever small project had caught his attention. He'd waved her off with a kiss and a smile that morning, reminding her to enjoy the day. He always did. Their marriage was comfortable after all these years, yet the spark had never faded. If anything, it had deepened since they'd made a life for themselves in this small community.

The library door opened and Mrs Talbot stepped inside, shaking rain from her umbrella.

'Morning, Maggie,' she said. 'I wonder when this rain will let up.'

'Morning,' Maggie replied. 'I thought it

might have been about to earlier. You're out and about early.'

Mrs Talbot smiled. 'Thought I'd return these before I forgot.' She placed a neat stack of books on the counter. Maggie glanced at the titles, noting the mix of fiction and local history. Mrs Talbot looked a bit distracted.

'Everything all right?' Maggie asked, scanning the returns.

'Yes, of course,' Mrs Talbot said quickly, then hesitated. 'Have you seen Arthur lately?'

Maggie paused. 'Arthur?'

'Yes. He's usually in town by now, isn't he? And when I walked past the café, he wasn't at his table.'

Maggie considered this. Arthur Blake was a regular fixture at the café. Same table, same seat, every morning. She realised he hadn't been there this morning.

'I don't think so,' she said. 'Not today.'

Mrs Talbot frowned. 'Probably nothing,' she said, too quickly. 'He's not young anymore. Could be under the weather.'

'Possibly,' Maggie agreed.

Mrs Talbot gathered her umbrella and left, the bell chiming softly behind her. Maggie knew she would do a spot of shopping, visit the café for tea and scones, and return later to borrow new books so she wouldn't have to carry them so far. Her routine was predictable, like so many others in town.

She made a mental note to check on Arthur later.

The morning passed quietly. A few patrons drifted in and out. Maggie helped a child find a book about rivers for a school project, checked out *All the Rivers Run* for Mrs Felton, and resisted the urge to smile at the coincidence.

She spent some time organising a box of donated papers for the Historical Society, setting aside a photograph she hadn't seen before. The river appeared in it too, winding behind a group of people whose faces had faded with time. Now this was getting just a little odd. She sighed. She would look at it properly on the weekend.

At lunchtime, she closed the library and walked home. Martin was at the table when she arrived, examining a small wooden box, running his fingers over the edges. Maggie slipped off her shoes and sat at the kitchen table.

'Lunch?' he asked.

'Please,' Maggie said.

As they ate together, Maggie told him about the river, about Mrs Talbot's question. Martin listened, nodding.

'Probably nothing,' he said eventually.

'Probably,' Maggie agreed. 'That salad was delicious, thanks, love.'

She put on her shoes again, kissed Martin's cheek and headed back to work.

The afternoon in the library was quiet. Between customers, Maggie worked on a jigsaw puzzle she had left on the sideboard. It was a muted landscape, soft greens and blues. She fitted a piece into place and stepped back, letting the picture reveal itself at its own pace. She found jigsaws calming, and they helped settle her very active mind.

Later that afternoon, she walked home along the river again. The water had risen a fraction more. She stood for a moment, watching the current tug at the bank, the water swirling, with its ebb and flow, ever so gently rearranging the debris on the banks. Something about it unsettled her, though she couldn't think why. She always trusted her instincts, even when she couldn't explain them.

By the time she turned for home, Maggie had the distinct feeling that Wattle River was hiding something.

She wasn't sure what, but she suspected it would not be for much longer.

Chapter Two

Maggie woke before the alarm and lay still, listening to the house. Martin's breathing beside her was slow and even, a steady presence that grounded her more than she cared to admit. She stared at the ceiling for a moment, then swung her legs out of bed and stood. Lying there any longer would only give her thoughts more room than they deserved, and work was waiting.

She dressed quietly and moved into the kitchen, filling the kettle and setting out two mugs without thinking about it. The small rituals helped keep her hands busy. Martin joined her while the water heated, already talking about the wooden box he'd been working on in the shed. One corner refused to sit flush, no matter how carefully he measured it.

'I think the timber's warped,' he said, turning the idea over aloud. 'Or it could just be me.'

'Or the joint's off by a fraction,' Maggie suggested.

He smiled. 'That's what I'm hoping. Easier fix.'

She listened while he talked it through, nodding, asking questions at the right moments. It helped, hearing him focus on something tangible, something that could be adjusted and made right. Still, when she reached for her coat, he studied her face a little more closely than usual.

'You're distracted,' he said.

'I don't think so,' Maggie replied, then paused. 'Well. Maybe a little.'

He didn't push. 'Arthur.'

'Yes.'

'He's probably fine.'

'I know,' she said, and meant it. Mostly.

She kissed his cheek and stepped outside.

The town was easing into the morning as she walked briskly towards the cafe. Her morning coffee would help perk her up after a restless night. Everything looked as it always did, and that unsettled her. When something was wrong in a small town, it rarely announced itself.

'Good morning, Helen.' Maggie greeted the café owner.

'Morning, Maggie. Your usual will be just a moment. I'm training a new barista this morning. This is Claire.' The young girl waved as she prepared Maggie's caramel latte with light milk, just as Helen had instructed.

'Still no Arthur?' Maggie enquired

casually.

'No, and it's been a few days now. Should someone go check on him, you think?'

'Maybe,' replied Maggie. 'But I'm sure it's fine. Probably just all this rain keeping him indoors.' It sounded plausible, but she still couldn't shake her feeling of unease.

At the library, Maggie unlocked the door and stepped inside. The quiet met her immediately, clean and expectant. She switched on the lights, opened the blinds, and began preparing for the day. A children's reading session was scheduled for mid-morning, so she laid out the books she'd chosen in the reading corner. Familiar favourites sat alongside one new title she hoped would spark interest. She arranged the small chairs, smoothed the rug, then checked the local history room sign-in sheet, as she always did.

Arthur's name was not there. For several

days

She closed the book and moved on.

The first patrons arrived soon after opening. Maggie scanned returns, answered questions, helped a woman find large-print books for her sister, and reassured a teenager hovering uncertainly near the computers. The library filled with low voices and quiet movement, and for a while, the unease loosened its grip, familiarity calming her.

At ten o'clock, parents and children gathered in the reading corner. There were eight today, more than usual. Some wriggled with impatience, while others watched her closely as she settled into the low chair with a book. Maggie waited until they settled, then began to read, adjusting her pace instinctively and allowing the children to interrupt with questions and observations.

She enjoyed this part of her job. The

library felt different during story time, warmer somehow, more alive, and definitely louder. It reminded her that stories weren't meant only to be read silently but also to be shared, discussed, and questioned.

Halfway through the book, a boy raised his hand. 'Where's the old man?' he asked.

Maggie smiled gently. 'Which old man?' she asked, biding her time to come up with a suitable answer.

'The one with the funny hat,' he said, pointing toward the window. 'He always sits there and listens.'

'I think you mean Arthur,' Maggie said.

'Yes,' the boy said. 'He told me about the car he used to have in the olden days. He said he'd bring a photo today.'

One of the parents laughed, quick and sharp. 'Alright, let Maggie finish the story.'

Maggie did, but the moment stayed with

her. Arthur had promised something. A photo. He had planned to come back, yet he wasn't here.

When the session ended, coats were gathered, and children were shepherded toward the door. One parent lingered behind, lowering her voice.

'Arthur usually comes in after story time,' she said. 'He likes to sit near the window.'

'Yes,' Maggie said.

'He's not unwell, is he?'

'I haven't heard anything,' Maggie replied. 'I expect he'll be back soon.'

The woman nodded, unconvinced, and left.

Maggie tidied the reading corner slowly, stacking the books, folding the rug, and returning the chairs to their places. The library felt suddenly emptier now that the children were gone, but it was also a relief not to have to make up excuses for Arthur's absence.

Late morning brought a steady stream of visitors. Maggie helped a book club regular track down a missing copy, answered questions about interlibrary loans, and accepted a box of donated materials from the Historical Society. She paused when she read the label.

Arthur Bell.

She set the box aside and continued working, although her attention drifted back to it again and again.

Just before lunch, Mrs Talbot returned a book and lingered at the counter.

'No sign of Arthur?' she asked. 'Even for the kiddies' reading time?'

'No.'

Mrs Talbot pursed her lips. 'That's not like him.'

'No.'

'Well,' she said briskly, 'I'm sure there's a

sensible explanation.'

Maggie smiled politely and watched her leave.

At lunchtime, Maggie locked up briefly and chose to eat on the bench near the library rather than walk home. She wanted the quiet and the vantage point. It was undercover from the rain, but she could still enjoy some fresh air while she ate her sandwiches. People passed, some stopping to chat, others hurrying on. Helen from the café waved as she walked by. Maggie waved back.

When she returned inside, she opened the donation box. Inside were neatly sorted papers, several photographs, and a slim notebook. Maggie recognised it immediately.

Arthur's notebook. He always carried it with him, tucked carefully into his bag. She sat down and opened it. Now that she thought about it, had he had this with him the last time he was at the library? Actually, when was that?

The pages were filled with dates, names, and references. Council meetings. Land titles. Notes written in Arthur's careful hand. Maggie read slowly, absorbing the pattern of his thinking. He cross-referenced everything. Margins were used sparingly, only when something needed emphasis. Symbols marked follow-ups. This was not idle curiosity. Arthur had been working toward something. But what?

Halfway through, she noticed the break.

A section was missing. Pages torn out cleanly, not ripped or damaged, but removed deliberately. The surrounding entries referenced a meeting that should have been documented, a parcel of land she recognised by name, and a note written twice, as if Arthur had wanted to be sure he didn't forget it.

Maggie closed the notebook.

She sat there for a long moment, hands

resting on the cover, aware of a faint shift inside herself. Arthur had not been careless. And whatever he had been working on, someone else had been involved.

Maggie slid the notebook into her desk drawer. She suddenly thought of locking it. She never had, but something told her this notebook held a connection to Arthur's strange disappearance.

The afternoon book club arrived just after two. It was a lively group, opinionated and prone to digression, and Maggie enjoyed guiding the discussion back on track when it wandered. Halfway through, Arthur's name came up again.

'He hasn't been in,' Joan said, reaching for another chocolate biscuit. 'I thought he'd have plenty to say about this one.' 'He always did,' Fred replied. 'Never agreed with me, mind.'

'That was half the fun,' someone else said.

A woman Maggie hadn't expected to speak to waved a dismissive hand. 'He probably got bored.'

'That doesn't sound like Arthur,' Joan said.

'Well,' the woman replied lightly. 'People change.'

The comment landed oddly. A few people laughed. Others didn't.

The thing that stuck in Maggie's mind was the way they were talking about Arthur in the past tense.

'Has anyone checked on him?' Fred asked.

'I'm sure there's a reason,' the woman said quickly. 'We don't need to make a fuss.'

Maggie let the conversation move on, but she noted who steered it and who looked uncomfortable.

By closing time, Maggie felt tired in a way that had nothing to do with physical effort. She stacked chairs, tidied the meeting room, and locked the front door. For a moment, she stood with the keys in her hand, weighing her options. Her mind was running at a hundred miles an hour.

Going straight home would be easier, but she decided to take the longer way and go past Arthur's place.

Arthur's cottage was quiet when she reached it. She stopped at the gate, scanning the place without knowing exactly what she hoped to see. She stood there longer than she intended, then turned back in the other direction.

On the walk home, Maggie replayed the day in her head. Arthur's absence was now noticeable. His notebook sat in her drawer. Questions were quietly forming in the places where people gathered.

Whatever was happening no longer fit neatly into routine, and the more she thought about it, Arthur's cottage may hold answers. No lights. No sound. His car was gone.

Chapter Three

When Maggie arrived at the library the next morning, she felt a recurring sense of being slightly out of sync with the day. Something had shifted, not dramatically, not yet, but enough that she couldn't quite settle back into ordinary.

Inside, the library greeted her with its usual calm. She switched on the lights, opened the blinds, and set her bag under the desk. The familiar order of the space steadied her. Places that didn't change gave her room to think.

She carefully handled the initial tasks, returning books to their shelves, straightening a displaced chair, and inspecting the returns trolley. She only paused upon entering the local history room.

Arthur's notebook was still in her desk drawer. She hadn't taken it home. That had been a deliberate choice. Some things belonged in neutral spaces, at least at first. The library had always been a place where information was held without judgment, and Maggie intended to treat Arthur's work with the same respect he would have.

She unlocked the drawer, took out the notebook, and placed it on the desk in front of her. For a moment, she simply looked at it, resisting the urge to open it again. She already knew what was inside. Dates. Names. Gaps. Enough to tell her that Arthur had been doing more than satisfying idle curiosity. His systematic nature was evident on every page. She slid the notebook back into the drawer and locked it. Today, she decided, was not about documents. It was about people.

The first visitors arrived soon after

opening. Maggie greeted them as usual, scanning returns and answering questions, letting the morning's rhythm immerse her. A woman she recognised from the book club stopped to ask about a new release. A man looking for old maps lingered near the history shelves, flipping through folders with careful hands. Maggie noticed the way he glanced toward the counter before asking his questions, as if measuring how much attention he might attract. She realised she was treating everything and everyone suspiciously. She helped him find what he was looking for and returned to her desk.

Arthur's absence had a different feel today. Yesterday, it had been remarked on in fragments, noticed in passing. Today, people were watching Maggie's reactions more closely. Not openly, but enough for her to feel it.

Late morning brought a lull in foot traffic,

which Maggie usually welcomed. She was reshelving returns when the front door opened, and the familiar bell chimed.

Helen Carter stepped inside, a takeaway cup balanced carefully in one hand, her handbag hooked over her arm.

'Well, hello there,' Maggie said, smiling.

Returning the smile, Helen lifted the cup slightly. 'You didn't come in this morning.'

'I didn't get the chance.'

'I noticed.' Helen crossed the floor and set the cup gently on the counter. 'Caramel latte. Light milk.'

Maggie paused, her hands still resting on a row of spines. She walked over and wrapped her fingers around the cup, warmth seeping into her palms. 'You didn't have to do that, but thank you so much. I'm glad you did.'

'I know I didn't,' Helen said. 'But you always come in. When you don't, I notice.'

Maggie gave a small, thoughtful smile. 'That seems to be the theme lately.'

Helen leaned against the counter, lowering her voice. 'People are noticing things they don't usually pay attention to.'

'Like routines?' Maggie asked.

Helen nodded. 'Exactly like that.'

Her gaze drifted briefly toward the local history room before returning to Maggie. 'Arthur has never missed two days in a row.'

'No,' Maggie said. 'He hasn't.'

Helen hesitated, then went on. 'Yesterday I told myself I was being silly. Today, people are asking me if I've heard anything. As if the café knows everything.'

Maggie took a sip of the coffee. It tasted exactly right. 'Sometimes it does.'

Helen smiled faintly. 'That's what worries me.'

There was a pause, not uncomfortable, but

weighted.

'Did he ever mention what he was looking into?' Maggie asked, keeping her tone light.

Helen frowned. 'Not directly. He talked about the town. About things changing. Said some decisions were made too quickly back then. But he never said what.'

'Did he seem concerned?'

'No.' Helen shook her head. 'Focused. Careful. Like he'd already lined everything up in his mind.'

She straightened. 'Anyway, I'd better get back. I just wanted to check on you. You look like someone who missed her morning coffee.'

Maggie smiled. 'That's probably because I did.'

'If you hear anything,' Helen said, reaching for her bag, 'let me know. People trust you.'

After she left, Maggie stood quietly for a

moment, coffee in hand.

Helen had noticed her absence and Arthur's. Others were noticing too. Once routines changed, they were hard to ignore.

Not long after, Mrs Talbot approached the counter with a book tucked neatly under her arm.

'Good morning,' Maggie said.

Mrs Talbot smiled. 'I was hoping you'd be here. Have you heard anything new?'

'About Arthur?' Maggie asked.

'Yes.'

'Nothing confirmed,' Maggie said carefully. 'But people are asking questions.'

Mrs Talbot nodded. 'As they should.'

The library was quieter now; the earlier rush having eased. Maggie chose not to let the moment pass.

'Do you know if Arthur was speaking to anyone in particular?' she asked. 'About his research?'

Mrs Talbot stiffened slightly. 'What do you mean?'

'Did he ever mention working with someone?' Maggie clarified.

Mrs Talbot considered this, then shook her head. 'Arthur was private, careful, and he liked to be certain before sharing things.'

'That sounds like him,' Maggie said.

Mrs Talbot leaned closer. 'Be careful, Maggie. Curiosity has a way of making people uncomfortable.'

Maggie smiled politely. 'It always has.'

After Mrs Talbot left, Maggie found it harder to settle. The library felt different, as if it were listening along with her. She reminded herself that she was still doing her job. Asking questions was part of that. Libraries existed to support inquiry, after all.

On a whim, she picked up the phone and

dialled Arthur's landline. It rang out.

At lunchtime, she locked the door and ate at her desk, using the quiet to think. The question she had asked Helen replayed in her mind, simple but deliberate. She had moved from noticing to asking, and she knew it.

When the library reopened, a familiar figure walked in almost immediately.

Evelyn Crowe moved with confidence. Her hair was neatly styled, her posture upright, and her expression composed. She carried a folder under one arm and smiled at Maggie.

'Maggie,' she said warmly. 'I hoped I'd catch you.'

'Good afternoon, Evelyn,' Maggie replied. 'What can I help you with?'

'I'm looking for some historical records,' Evelyn said, placing the folder on the desk. 'Council meeting minutes. From some years ago.'

'Do you know which years?' Maggie asked, her interest suddenly piqued.

Evelyn waved a hand lightly. 'The late nineties, perhaps. Early two-thousands. I'm helping prepare a retrospective piece for the historical society.'

'That's quite a range,' Maggie said. 'Is there a particular topic?'

'Land use,' Evelyn replied smoothly. 'Zoning decisions. Infrastructure.'

Maggie nodded and stood to retrieve the relevant indexes.

'I hear you've been very busy,' Evelyn added casually. 'People have been coming to you with questions.'

'People tend to do that in libraries,' Maggie said.

Evelyn smiled. 'Some questions are better left unanswered.'

Maggie turned back to her. 'Unanswered

questions tend to linger.'

Evelyn studied her for a moment, the smile never quite leaving her face. 'That depends on who's asking.'

They worked through the records together. Maggie noticed how efficiently Evelyn moved through the pages, how little time she spent on sections that should have required closer reading.

When they finished, Evelyn closed the folder. 'Thank you. This has been most helpful.'

'I'm glad,' Maggie said, smiling gently. Something about this woman left her uneasy.

Evelyn gathered her things, then paused. 'May I offer a word of advice?'

Maggie met her gaze. 'Of course.'

'This town values harmony,' Evelyn said. 'People have long memories, but they also protect what matters to them. It's important not to stir things unnecessarily.'

Maggie chose her words with care, the unease increasing. 'Truth has a way of surfacing eventually.'

Evelyn smiled again, though this time it didn't reach her eyes. 'I hope you're right.'

After she left, Maggie remained behind the desk, her thoughts unsettled. The exchange had been polite, even generous. That made it more dangerous.

She retrieved Arthur's notebook from the drawer and opened it to the back pages. Her eyes moved through the familiar columns of dates and references, clearer now than the first time she'd read them.

Evelyn Crowe. She hadn't noticed how many times the name had appeared before. Maggie turned to the page she had memorised— the one with the missing section, the torn edge still slightly raised. Just before the gap, in Arthur's careful hand.

Ask E.C.

She looked at it for a long moment, then closed the notebook.

The afternoon passed uneventfully, but the sense of unease did not fade. By closing time, Maggie felt drained in a way that had nothing to do with the day's work.

She locked the doors, turned off the lights, and stood for a moment in the stillness.

She had asked her first deliberate question. She had been told, just as deliberately, to stop.

As she walked home, Maggie knew with certainty that she wouldn't.

Chapter Four

By the fourth day of Arthur Bell's absence, the town had stopped pretending nothing was wrong. No one said it outright, but unease surfaced in small, careful ways. People paused before answering simple questions. Conversations softened as someone new stepped closer. What had begun as quiet concern now carried weight, as if everyone were waiting for something to shift. Maggie felt it as she moved behind the library desk. The morning was already underway. A stack of returns waited to be processed. A low murmur of voices drifted in from the shelves near the front windows. It should have felt ordinary, but there was a sense of alertness, as though the town itself were paying closer attention to how she went about her day.

She logged into the records system and brought up the council archive index, scanning it with a practised eye. Maggie was not looking for anything dramatic. Arthur had never worked that way. He had been patient and precise, following threads until they either revealed something useful or quietly disappeared. She worked in much the same way.

Dates repeated. Language shifted. Certain meetings were carefully summarised, while others were recorded in frustratingly vague terms. There were no obvious gaps, nothing that would alarm someone skimming the pages, but when Maggie followed the same sequence Arthur had traced, a pattern emerged. Agendas referenced but not included. Decisions noted without explanation. A cluster of entries that ended abruptly, then resumed months later under a softened heading.

She began to take notes, keeping them factual and restrained. Interpretation could wait. Experience had taught her that conclusions reached too quickly were rarely right. Maggie loved a good notebook and always preferred to write things down rather than do it electronically. By mid-morning, the library was full. Maggie moved through her usual tasks, helping a man find a pruning guide, directing a visitor to the local history shelves, and answering a question about borrowing limits. Each interaction was polite and unremarkable, yet she noticed how often eyes lingered on her face. How conversations faltered as she passed. Why was she suddenly the centre of attention?

Arthur's name was not spoken, but it was clearly on people's minds.

Just before ten, a woman Maggie recognised from the historical society approached the desk, pamphlet in hand.

'Maggie,' she said warmly. 'I was hoping to ask for your assistance.'

'Good morning,' Maggie replied. 'What can I help you with?'

'We're planning a small exhibition,' the woman said. 'Something positive. A celebration of how far the town's come. I wondered if you might suggest a few suitable pieces.'

'Of course,' Maggie said. 'Is there a particular period you're focusing on?'

'Oh, the early days,' the woman replied quickly. 'Founding families. Major milestones.'

Maggie nodded. 'I'll see what we have.'

The woman smiled, then added lightly, 'Probably best not to reopen old debates, though. People prefer to remember the good things.'

Maggie met her gaze, a little puzzled. 'History usually includes all of it.'

'Yes,' the woman said, her smile

tightening just slightly. 'But not everything needs revisiting.'

After she left, Maggie remained still for a moment, the pamphlet resting on the counter. It was the third conversation in as many days that carried the same quiet message, each delivered with concern rather than confrontation.

The message was always the same. Let it be. Don't unsettle things. Leave the past where it was.

At eleven, Maggie made her first deliberate move.

She printed a formal access request for a small set of council records Arthur had referenced repeatedly. The request was narrow, precise, and entirely appropriate. She logged it, attached the relevant reference numbers, and submitted it through the proper channel. There was nothing provocative about it. Nothing that should have raised concern.

The phone rang just after midday.

'Good afternoon, Wattle River Library. Maggie Ellis speaking,' she answered in her usual friendly manner.

'Maggie, it's Daniel from council.'

'Yes,' she said. 'Thanks for calling.'

'I'm ringing about your request.'

'That was fast work.'

Daniel hesitated. 'Some of those records aren't held on-site anymore.'

'I know,' Maggie said. 'That's why I followed the retrieval process.'

'Yes, but retrieval can take time.'

'I understand.'

'And there may be some restrictions.'

Maggie leaned back slightly. 'Restrictions on council minutes? Aren't they a matter for public record?'

'Well,' Daniel said, sounding uncomfortable, 'certain files are considered sensitive.'

'On what basis?'

'Context,' he replied quickly. 'The potential for misinterpretation.'

Maggie let the silence stretch. 'They're public records.'

'Yes, but I'll need to check with my supervisor.'

'Of course,' Maggie said evenly. 'Please let me know.'

When she ended the call, she stayed where she was, absorbing what had not quite been said. There had been no refusal, no explanation, just a gentle slowing of the process justified by procedure and red tape. It was effective. And it was deliberate.

The afternoon passed with a subdued intensity. Maggie continued helping patrons, answering questions, and guiding people through the shelves, all while noting subtle shifts in behaviour. A man she greeted daily avoided her eye and hurried out without returning his book. Two women fell silent mid-sentence as she approached. Was she imagining it?

Around two o'clock, a woman Maggie did not recognise came to the desk, her expression uncertain.

'I was told you might be able to help me,' she said.

'Certainly. Are you looking for a particular book?' Maggie asked.

'Records,' the woman replied. 'Property ones. Old ones.'

Maggie gestured to the chair opposite her. 'Tell me what you're looking for.'

The woman sat, clutching her handbag. 'My brother and I inherited land from our father. Or we thought we had. Somewhere along the line, the boundaries changed. The paperwork doesn't match what he always said.'

'Have you spoken to the council?' Maggie asked.

'We were told everything was in order.'

'And is it?'

The woman hesitated. 'I don't know.'

Maggie pulled out the relevant maps and files, guiding her carefully through them without commentary. She watched as the woman traced the lines, her brow furrowing.

'This doesn't make sense,' she murmured.

'No,' Maggie agreed quietly.

When the woman left, shaken but grateful, Maggie sat back and let out a slow breath. Arthur's work came into sharper focus. He had not been searching aimlessly. He had been discovering where official records and everyday reality no longer aligned. '

Later in the afternoon, Mrs Talbot paused at the desk, lowering her voice.

'I heard Arthur's daughter's been in touch with the police,' she said.

Maggie kept her expression neutral. 'Oh?'

'They did a welfare check. Went by the cottage. No sign of him.'

'And his car?' Maggie asked.

'Gone,' Mrs Talbot said. 'That's what's worrying people.'

A missing car changed the shape of things. It allowed for sensible explanations while opening new questions. Had Arthur driven away, or had someone else driven for him?

The police presence remained distant, implied rather than visible. Enough to reassure some, not enough to satisfy others.

Daniel called again just before closing.

'My supervisor's asked that you submit a revised request,' he said. 'Specifying exact documents and intended use.'

'I've already done that.'

'Yes, but this one will need to go before the records committee.'

'Which meets when?'

'Next week.'

Maggie smiled faintly. 'I'll submit whatever you need.'

After the call, she sat quietly, the nature of the resistance now unmistakable. Not loud or aggressive, but organised. Polite. Collective.

When she locked the library doors and turned off the lights, the building felt steady and unchanged. That steadied her in return. The records were still here, even if people were trying to delay access to them.

At home, Martin was in the shed, sanding a piece of timber. He looked up as she approached.

'Long day?' he asked.

'Revealing,' Maggie said.

He studied her face. 'You're not going to

stop, are you?'

'No,' she answered honestly. 'I can't.'

They did not linger over dinner. Later, Maggie set up her jigsaw puzzle on the sideboard, fitting a few pieces together without focusing on the emerging picture. She liked the patience it required, the way meaning only appeared once enough pieces were in place.

That was how Arthur had worked.

And how she would, too.

By the time Maggie switched off the lights and went to bed, she understood one thing clearly. Asking questions had changed how the town responded to her.

She was no longer just noticing.

She was being noticed.

And she was not willing to look away.

Chapter Five

Maggie had almost reached the corner when her phone rang. The number was private. She hesitated, then answered. The voice on the other end paused before speaking, measured and deliberate in a way that immediately set her on edge.

'Maggie Ellis?'

'Yes. This is Maggie Ellis'

'This is Constable Reid. I'm calling in relation to Arthur Bell.'

Maggie closed her eyes briefly. 'All right.'

'We're just making contact with people who know him well,' the constable said. 'Routine enquiries.'

'I understand.'

'You'd see him regularly?'

'Yes. Most mornings. Either at the café or in his favourite seat in the library.'

'And when did you last see him?'

'Earlier this week. At the café.'

There was a brief silence, the sound of paper shifting. 'We've confirmed he wasn't at home when officers attended, and his vehicle isn't at the property.'

Maggie absorbed that. She had known it already, but hearing it spoken officially made it feel somehow more solid.

'Has he ever mentioned plans to travel?' the constable asked.

'No,' Maggie said. 'Arthur was not impulsive.'

'Thank you. If you hear from him, or if anything comes to mind, please let us know.'

'Absolutely. Thank you.'

The call ended without ceremony. No

urgency. No reassurance. Just enough contact to confirm that Arthur's absence now belonged to more than the town. It was official. The police were involved and Maggie's senses heightened further.

Maggie arrived at the library with a sharpened sense of purpose. She did not linger on routine. She logged into the records system and pulled up the council archive index again, cross-checking entries she had already flagged. What she wanted now was confirmation. Something that proved Arthur had been close to a conclusion, not simply circling questions. But what?

The morning unfolded steadily. Patrons came and went. A mother settled her children in the reading corner for story time, and Maggie read aloud with her usual calm focus, choosing a book about maps and journeys. The children listened, absorbed, unaware of how closely the story mirrored her own quiet search for direction.

Afterwards, one of the mothers lingered.

'Arthur used to help my dad,' she said. 'With paperwork. He said Arthur explained things no one else would.'

Maggie nodded. 'He was very thorough.'

'He said some of it didn't make sense,' the woman added. 'The council stuff.'

Maggie made a mental note. 'Did your father keep any of that paperwork?'

'I think so. I can check.'

'Please do,' Maggie said. 'That would be helpful.'

By late morning, Maggie's email notification chimed.

Her records request had been acknowledged again. Further review was required. Access would be discussed at the committee level due to historical sensitivity.

Council matters were traditionally dealt with at a snail's pace, but this was ridiculous.

And still no timeline. Funny that.

She printed the message and added it to her folder. Delay was now unmistakable.

Instead of returning to the archives, Maggie turned to the donated materials Arthur had been cataloguing. She worked through them carefully, not rushing, allowing patterns to emerge on their own terms. She had learned from Arthur's notes that patience revealed more than persistence ever could. That was when she found the exercise book again.

This time, she took it to the desk and opened it fully.

The handwriting was consistent throughout. Dates were listed in sequence. Names appeared repeatedly, sometimes struck through and replaced. Lot numbers were recorded alongside short annotations.

She copied several entries into her notebook, aligning them with council references she already knew. The discrepancies were subtle yet deliberate. Amendments noted here were absent from official records. Decisions seemed to change without explanation.

And it was very clear that Arthur had not been guessing. He had been verifying.

Mid-afternoon, Maggie became aware that she was no longer alone. Her attention had been fully engaged in the exercise book when a small cough made her look up.

Evelyn Crowe stood near the desk, waiting politely.

'Maggie,' she said. 'I hope I'm not interrupting.' How long had she been standing there?

'Not at all,' Maggie replied, closing the exercise book and doing her best not to appear flustered.

'I wanted to check in with you,' Evelyn said. 'There's been a great deal of concern about Arthur.'

'Yes. He's very well-liked about town. A lovely man'

'I understand the police have been in contact.'

'They have.' How did this woman know everything?

Evelyn nodded. 'It's reassuring to know things are being handled properly. Situations like this can become unsettling if too many people involve themselves.'

She met Evelyn's gaze. 'Arthur's work involved helping people understand records.'

'And records can be misread,' Evelyn said gently. 'Context matters.'

'So does accuracy.'

Evelyn smiled, unconvincingly. 'Of course. I simply hope no one causes unnecessary worry while things are being clarified.'

After Evelyn left, Maggie remained at the desk, replaying the conversation. Evelyn had known the police had made contact. She had known Maggie was looking into records. None of that was a coincidence. Was it a threat? And if so, why?

That evening, Maggie walked past Arthur's cottage again.

The gate was closed. The letterbox was empty. Someone had collected the mail. A neighbour paused in their driveway, watching her openly. She smiled and gave a brief wave. It was not returned before the man disappeared inside his house.

Arthur was no longer just missing. His absence was being noticed in ways it hadn't been before. And so was Maggie.

***

At home, Maggie laid her notes out on the table, aligning dates and names until a clear sequence began to form. It was not enough to prove anything yet, but it was enough to confirm one thing.

Arthur had been close.

Close enough for systems to resist. Close enough for people to intervene. Close enough to disappear.

Maggie closed her notebook and turned off the light, her resolve steady and deliberate.

She would continue carefully. There was no need to draw unwanted attention.

Arthur had trusted process.

So would she.

Chapter Six

Maggie was midway through re-shelving a stack of returns when her phone vibrated in her pocket.

She ignored it at first. Phones buzzed constantly, often for reasons that could wait. She slid the last book into place, adjusted the row so the spines sat evenly, then checked the screen. The number was private. Her gut instinct told her this was important and likely not a friendly check-in.

She did not answer immediately. Instead, she stepped into the small workroom at the back of the library, closing the door behind her. She hit the accept call button.

'Maggie Ellis speaking.'

There was a pause, brief but deliberate, before the voice on the other end responded. 'Mrs Ellis, this is Constable Reid.'

'Hello, Constable,' Maggie said.

'I'm calling to let you know that Arthur Bell has been located.'

Maggie closed her eyes. The wording mattered. Located was not the same as safe.

'Where is he?' she asked.

Another pause followed, longer this time. She could hear faint movement in the background, the rustle of paper, a quiet shift as though the constable had stepped aside.

'Downstream from the bridge,' he said. 'Near the riverbank.'

Maggie rested her hand against the bench, her fingers pressing lightly into the laminate.

'And?' she said.

'I'm sorry to say that he's deceased.'

The words arrived calmly, without

emphasis, and they hit her, as if in slow motion. Maggie did not speak at once. She let the information sink in fully before responding. Her stomach tightened, and she held her breath.

'I see,' she managed quietly. This news was somehow anticipated, but felt suddenly so heavy and final. It hit her harder than expected.

'We felt it was best you heard directly,' the constable continued. 'Given your connection to Mr Bell.'

'Thank you for telling me. I do appreciate the courtesy.'

'There will be further contact later. For now, we're asking people to avoid the area.'

'Yes,' Maggie said. 'Of course.'

The call ended quietly. No sirens. No urgency. Just a statement of fact, delivered with care.

Maggie remained where she was, her palm still flat against the bench. Arthur Bell was dead. She had prepared herself for this moment without admitting it, but that preparation did not soften the impact. It only meant she was not surprised by the direction her thoughts took.

Arthur had been missing. His absence had been explained away as old age, illness, or the weather, and now he had been found. The progression unsettled Maggie, each step feeling like part of a pattern she hadn't wanted to see. Arthur was dead, and there was more to this tragedy than met the eye. She just knew it.

She drew in a slow breath, straightened her shoulders, and stepped back into the main library. For the first time she could remember, she just wanted to leave the building. It was too hot, too claustrophobic. She needed fresh air.

Two patrons stood at the desk, waiting patiently. Maggie crossed to them, her expression more composed than she felt, her voice steady.

'I'm afraid I'll need to close early this afternoon,' she said. 'There's been an emergency.'

They exchanged a glance and nodded immediately. No one asked for details. In Wattle River, news often arrived before explanation, and people recognised the signs. Maggie moved through the library, announcing the closure, helping people gather their belongings, guiding a pair of children back to their mother, locking computers and switching off lights. The routine steadied her slightly. It gave her something practical to focus on while her mind continued to turn over what she had just been told.

By the time the last patron left, the quiet felt smothering.

Maggie stood alone near the desk, taking in the space she knew so well. Arthur had spent countless hours here, seated at one of the long tables, his notebooks spread carefully around him. He had asked questions that others skimmed past, followed references that led nowhere obvious, and treated the records with patience and respect.

Now he was gone.

She locked the door and stepped outside into the fresh air she craved. It felt better, but she fought back tears that threatened to spill.

The town had already begun to respond.

A small group stood near the general store, voices low and urgent. Someone stopped speaking when Maggie passed. Others nodded solemnly, their expressions set somewhere between shock and resignation. News moved quickly here, carried by glances and half-heard remarks, and people sensed when something final had occurred.

Maggie did not head straight home.

Instead, she walked towards the bridge,

slowing as she drew closer. A police vehicle was parked well to the side of the road, unobtrusive, its presence understated. There were no barriers, no tape, nothing to mark the spot beyond a quiet sense of caution. A few police were present, but there was little activity, given that a body had just been discovered.

She stopped at a distance, her gaze drawn to the water below. It moved steadily, unremarkable in its flow, giving nothing away.

Arthur had been found nearby. Not in the water, but close to it. The distinction lodged in Maggie's mind. It suggested hesitation, or a plan that had not been carried through. Whatever had happened, it had ended before concealment could be completed.

When she turned away, she saw Helen standing a short distance back, her face pale.

'I heard,' Helen said quietly.

Maggie nodded. 'I'm sorry,' as she briefly

embraced the other woman

Helen swallowed. 'So am I. He was a good man.'

They stood together for a moment, neither of them speaking. There was nothing useful to add.

At home, Martin met Maggie at the door.

He did not ask questions. He simply wrapped his arms around her and held her while the weight of the day finally caught up.

'They found him,' Maggie said, and silent tears finally fell as she nestled into her husband's embrace. He was always her safe place.

'I know,' Martin replied softly. 'Everyone knows.'

She pulled back, wiping her eyes. 'Near the river.'

Martin nodded. 'That's what people are saying.'

'They didn't say how,' Maggie added. 'Or when.'

Martin did not press.

They sat together for a while, the quiet between them steady rather than strained. Eventually, Maggie stood and moved to the kitchen bench, absently rinsing a mug of tea she had barely touched.

Her thoughts kept circling back to the same questions, turning over the reasons for Arthur's presence, the timing of it all, why everything had come to a head when it did, and the sense that none of it had been random.

She thought of the exercise book. Of the careful handwriting and amended lot numbers. Of the council records that had suddenly become sensitive. Of the way people had begun to caution her about curiosity the moment she followed Arthur's path. It did not sit well with her.

Arthur had been careful. 'Methodical' was the word constantly used to describe him. He would not have put himself in danger without understanding the risk. Which meant he had known he was close to something that mattered.

And yet his car was still missing.

That detail refused to leave her mind. If Arthur had been found near the river, how had he got there? Why had his car not been located at the river, or why had it not been at the cottage?

Maggie did not leap to conclusions. She knew better than that. Still, the absence of the car sat awkwardly alongside everything else, a loose piece that did not fit the picture she was forming.

As evening fell over Wattle River, the town grew quieter than usual. Shops closed early. Lights flicked on behind curtains. The usual rhythm softened, replaced by something subdued and watchful.

Maggie stepped outside just before dark and walked to the end of the street. From there, she could see the bridge in the distance, its outline faint against the deepening sky. She did not picture Arthur there. She did not allow herself to do that. Instead, she focused on what he left unfinished.

The records he had worked through so carefully, the notes he had taken, and the people who had relied on him to help make sense of things they had long accepted without question. She also could not ignore the other side of it now, the people who had been unsettled by his work and who had wanted him to stop. In the days ahead, Arthur Bell's death would be spoken of carefully around town. There would be condolences offered in hushed tones, speculation kept deliberately vague, and quiet reminders that some things were better left alone. But for Maggie, the line had already been crossed. This was no longer a matter of mild concern or professional curiosity, nor was it simply about a disrupted routine or unanswered questions. Whatever had begun with Arthur did not end with him, and she was resolved to uncover the truth.

Arthur had been murdered. Now she just had to piece together the clues and prove it

Maggie turned back toward home, 'I will finish what you started Arthur. I will find the truth.'

Chapter Seven

By the time Maggie reached the library, the town had already decided what it wanted to believe.

It wasn't that people were cruel about Arthur Bell. They weren't. If anything, most of them were kinder than Maggie expected, offering quiet condolences to one another in the street, pausing outside shopfronts to talk about him in the past tense as if the word itself might keep the grief tidy. But beneath the sadness was something else, something that pressed at Maggie's nerves.

Relief. Relief that it had been simple. Relief that it had not been something worse. Relief that there was a neat explanation that didn't require anyone to look too hard at anything.

As Maggie unlocked the front door, she heard two women on the footpath behind her. 'Poor love,' one said. 'But at least it wasn't foul play.' 'No,' the other agreed. 'That's what they said. A turn. Heart. Something like that. He was getting on.'

'They've taken him to Taree, haven't they?'

'Post-mortem, but it's routine. That's what my cousin said. Routine.'

Routine. The word sat oddly in Maggie's mind. Nothing about a man being found dead near the river felt routine, no matter how many times someone repeated it.

Maggie turned on the lights inside the library, lifted the blinds, and worked through her opening tasks with steady hands. Returns, reservations, and the daily notices. She didn't rush, but she didn't linger either. She knew her habits well enough to recognise when her mind was circling and settling, seeking comfort in repetition.

By mid-morning, the first wave arrived. Parents with small children, older locals returning books, people dropping in for the computers. A few offered Maggie soft, careful condolences, as if the library came with a rule that grief had to be spoken quietly.

'You must be shocked,' a woman said at the counter, eyes wide with sincerity.

'It's sad,' Maggie replied, scanning the stack of picture books and keeping her voice level.

'He was such a fixture,' the woman continued. 'But these things happen. At least it's not… you know.'

Maggie looked up. 'Not what?'

The woman shifted, embarrassed. 'Not

anything sinister.'

Now, what would make you say that?

Maggie gave a small nod and returned her attention to the scanner. The woman left, satisfied, as though she'd done her part by naming what everyone else was thinking without quite saying.

Another patron, a man who rarely spoke beyond a greeting, paused at Maggie's desk. 'They told me it wasn't suspicious,' he said, as if reporting the weather.

'Who told you?'

'The police. Yesterday afternoon. They were just tying things up.' He seemed pleased by the phrasing. 'Tying things up.'

Maggie watched him go, feeling her stomach tighten. That was the problem. People wanted it tied up. A bow on top. A town of tidy endings.

She opened her desk drawer and took out

Arthur's notebook. The slim book lay in her hands, and a heaviness descended on her. She placed it on the table and opened it to the section she'd last seen. Dates, names and references. Small, precise handwriting. Cross-checks in the margins. Councillors' surnames, meeting minutes, land decisions, and those careful notations that Arthur seemed to use often.

Then, the gap. Several pages were missing, removed cleanly, the torn edge too neat to be an accident. Maggie ran her fingers lightly along the paper, not for comfort, but to test the reality of it again. Arthur would not have done that without a reason.

Did Arthur even do it? Who else had access to his notebook?

She flipped back a few pages and read more slowly this time. The writing was calm, not frantic. Arthur hadn't been panicking but focused on work. What unsettled Maggie the most was that his notes showed the calm patience of someone convinced that he had time on his side. She found the line again, written twice, as if he feared forgetting it.

Ask E.C.

Maggie closed the notebook and sat back. She didn't know who E.C. was, not for certain. She could guess it was Evelyn Crowe, but guessing was not evidence, and it was not her way. She slid the notebook back into the drawer and locked it. Some lines mattered, and some things needed to be protected until she understood what she was actually holding.

When she stepped back into the main library, a man was waiting near the counter. He was in plain clothes, but he carried himself like someone used to being listened to. Neat hair, practical shoes, a tidy folder in his hand. He didn't look like he belonged to the flow of Wattle River's morning errands. He looked more like a detective.

'Maggie Ellis?' he asked.

'Yes.'

He offered a brief, polite smile. 'Detective Senior Constable Rowan. I'm from Taree. I'm just following up on a few things.'

Maggie kept her face neutral. 'Following up on Arthur Bell?'

'Yes. Nothing alarming,' Rowan said quickly, as if he'd already learned what people needed to hear. 'It's being treated as non-suspicious, but there are always details to confirm. We like to be thorough.'

Thorough. Maggie almost smiled at the irony, but she didn't.

Rowan glanced around. 'Could we speak for a moment? Somewhere quiet?'

Maggie gestured toward the side desk near the window, where they could speak without being overheard but still within the public space. She wasn't interested in secrecy. She was interested in keeping things ordinary.

Rowan opened his folder. 'You work here. You'd have seen Arthur often.'

'Yes.'

'And you were aware he had an interest in local history.'

'Yes.'

Rowan's pen hovered over the paper. 'Was that interest casual, or… intense?'

Are you thinking what I'm thinking?

Maggie chose her words carefully. 'Arthur was careful. He liked facts. He liked records.'

'Did he ever mention being worried?'

'No.'

'Did he ever mention anyone giving him trouble?'

'No.'

Rowan nodded, as if he expected that. 'We've heard he'd been asking questions around town.'

'He asked questions,' Maggie replied. 'That doesn't mean he was in trouble.'

Rowan gave another polite smile. 'Exactly. A lot of people are connecting dots because of the timing.'

Maggie looked at him. 'Are you connecting dots?'

'Just doing my job,' Rowan said easily. 'Which, at the moment, is mostly ensuring there isn't something we've missed. But as I said, there's no indication of foul play. No struggle, no signs of an assault. The working assumption is that a medical episode occurred. Possibly compounded by the weather, the ground conditions, and the walk. The head wound is compatible with that theory'

Head wound?

Maggie kept her hands folded on the desk. 'And the notebook?'

Rowan blinked. 'The notebook?'

Maggie watched his face, the small flicker of surprise that came before he caught it. 'Arthur always carried a notebook.'

Rowan's pen paused. 'We're aware he wrote things down. But why would that have anything to do with his death? There wasn't a notebook found on his person'

Rowan continued, 'If you come across anything that suggests he was frightened or threatened, please contact Senior Constable Harris. Otherwise, I expect this will be finalised once the routine reports come back.'

Maggie nodded. 'Of course.'

Rowan closed his folder and stood. 'Thank you for your time.'

He left in the same manner he'd arrived, and Maggie watched the front door swing shut behind him. The interaction had been professional and ordinary. Routine.

There's that word again.

That was what worried her. If the system had already decided it was ordinary, then anything that wasn't would be smoothed away before it ever had a chance to be seen.

At lunch, Maggie didn't go home. She ate at her desk, dividing her attention between the patrons and the feeling that sat behind her ribs like a small pressure. She watched people come in, drop off books, and speak of Arthur in softened phrases.

'Such a shame.'

'At least he went quickly.'

'He wouldn't want a fuss.'

'He had a good life.'

Maggie nodded when she needed to, smiled when required, and kept the library running. The town needed that. It needed the normality of due dates, book recommendations, and children tugging at their parents' sleeves to look at the stickers in the reading corner.

The Local History Group gathered in the late afternoon. Unlike the Historical Society, which had its own committee, meetings, and a formal membership list, and was approached with a sense of reverence, the Local History Group was more informal. They met in the library's back room because that was where the materials were and because Maggie provided the space. Members sorted, catalogued, planned small displays, and assisted with questions from school students and curious visitors interested in the town's past. Comprising volunteers—local residents passionate about sharing town history—they were practical, preferring paper and order.

Arthur had been one of them, but today his chair would remain empty.

Maggie set out tea and a plate of biscuits.

Margaret Hill arrived first, as she often

did. Margaret was in her late sixties, hair neatly styled, cardigan buttoned, her handbag organised in a way that suggested she ran her life like a filing system. She had been involved with council matters for years. Officially retired, she still carried the authority of someone accustomed to being listened to.

'Hello, Maggie,' Margaret said, eyes taking in the room. 'Thank you for keeping this going.'

Maggie nodded. 'People need a space to talk and grieve together.'

'They do,' Margaret agreed.

Two others arrived behind her: Len, who had once worked at the council depot and still spoke as if he were giving a report, and Maureen, who had lived in Wattle River all her life and seemed to know the history of every house, every block of land, and every family connection. They settled at the table, shuffling papers, opening folders, and making small talk that circled around Arthur without touching him directly.

Then Maureen said what everyone was thinking. 'It's strange, isn't it, sitting here without him.'

Len cleared his throat. 'A shame. He was dedicated.'

Margaret folded her hands. 'Arthur cared about the town.'

'He cared about the truth,' Maggie said.

Margaret's gaze flicked to her. 'Yes. Of course. But there are ways of caring about truth that are useful, and ways that only unsettle people.'

Maggie held Margaret's gaze. 'Truth doesn't become less true because it makes people uncomfortable.'

Maureen glanced between them, suddenly alert. 'Arthur was researching some old council decisions,' she said carefully. 'That's what he told me.'

Len shifted in his chair. 'Lots of old decisions. People ask about things all the time.'

Maureen ignored him. 'He was looking at land records. And not just the ones people talk about.'

Margaret's tone remained calm. 'The town's land records have been reviewed plenty of times. Matters were resolved.'

Maggie reached for a folder and opened it, not because she needed the contents but because she needed the steady action. 'Arthur didn't think they were resolved.'

Len gave a short laugh. 'Arthur liked a mystery. He liked feeling like he'd found something.'

'That's not fair,' Maureen said sharply. 'Arthur wasn't a fool.'

'No one said he was,' Len replied, but his

voice carried irritation now.

Margaret lifted a hand. 'We can honour Arthur's memory without letting this become something it doesn't need to be.' She commanded attention with just a look.

Heat rose behind Maggie's eyes, not anger exactly, but that familiar sensation of being treated as if she were overreacting when she hadn't even raised her voice. She kept her tone steady. 'The police are treating his death as a medical episode.'

Margaret nodded. 'As they should, unless they find evidence otherwise.'

'And if they don't look for evidence?' Maggie asked. The question came out quieter than she intended.

Maureen stared at her. Len shifted again, uncomfortable. Margaret's expression stayed pleasant, but something in it cooled.

'Maggie,' Margaret said, 'it's

understandable to feel unsettled. You saw Arthur often. You were fond of him. But this is not the time to stir uncertainty. People are grieving.'

'People are repeating a version of events because it feels safer,' Maggie replied.

Margaret leaned slightly forward. 'People are choosing to move forward.'

Silence settled over the table for a moment, broken only by the soft rustle of paper as Maureen, deliberately, opened a folder and began sorting, as if to remind them why they were here.

Maggie took a breath and did the same. The meeting continued, but the shape of it had changed. Margaret steered the conversation away from Arthur whenever it drifted too close. Len became brisk and practical, speaking more than he needed to, filling space. Maureen stayed quiet, but her eyes kept lifting to Maggie's, as if asking a question she didn't dare say aloud.

Near the end, as they packed away, Margaret approached Maggie, where she stood by the shelves. 'You're doing good work here,' Margaret said, voice low enough that the others wouldn't hear. 'And I don't want to see you make trouble for yourself.'

Maggie kept her hands on the folder she was holding. 'I'm not trying to make trouble.'

'I know,' Margaret said, as though that was the problem. 'But intention doesn't matter as much as outcome. Small towns have long memories. People don't thank you for unsettling things they'd rather not think about.'

Maggie met her gaze. 'Arthur unsettled something.'

Margaret's smile tightened. 'Arthur had a habit of looking at things and assuming he saw what others missed. Sometimes that's admirable. Sometimes it's… unhelpful.'

Maggie's heart beat a fraction faster. 'Are you saying he was wrong?'

'I'm saying it's not the time,' Margaret replied. 'Let the police finish their routine checks. Let the town grieve. Don't go pulling at threads that have been tied off.'

Maggie's voice stayed calm. 'Threads don't stay tied off forever. They just get buried.'

Margaret's gaze held hers for a moment longer than was comfortable. Then she patted Maggie's arm lightly, a gesture that looked kind but felt like an instruction. 'Be sensible,' she said.

When the group left, the library quieted again. Maggie locked the meeting room and stood for a moment with her hand resting on the key, feeling the day's conversations in her body like static.

She returned to her desk and opened the drawer where she'd locked Arthur's notebook.

She did not take it out straight away. She sat and stared at the drawer, as if she could persuade herself that leaving it there would make her feel better, but it didn't.

She took the notebook out and opened it again. She read the same pages she'd read before, but this time she wasn't looking for meaning in the whole of it. She was looking for one thing: what Arthur had been close to when the pages disappeared. The entries around the gap referenced meeting minutes and land records, and one notation stood out because it was repeated. Ask E.C. Written twice, as if Arthur had promised himself he would do it, even if the conversation was uncomfortable.

Maggie closed the notebook and sat back.

E.C.

. Initials were easy. People with reputations were easier still. But she didn't allow herself to jump. Not yet. If she was going to do this, she would do it properly. The town had enough assumptions. It didn't need Maggie adding to them. She slid the notebook back into the drawer and locked it.

Then she did something she hadn't done before.

She opened Arthur's library account.

Arthur's borrowing history displayed on her screen: dates, titles, due dates, and returns. Maggie examined it carefully, remaining focused and attentive. Over the past month, she noted several local-history-related items had been checked out—council minutes, a collection of clippings, and a record book that was seldom borrowed due to its dullness, weight, and mostly containing numbers. However, one specific item stood out to her.

A volume of old council meeting minutes had been checked out and not returned. It wasn't overdue by much, but it sat on the list like a small gap. Maggie clicked into the details and frowned.

The return date had been manually adjusted. That was unusual.

Maggie's fingers hovered over the keyboard. Manual adjustments weren't forbidden. Sometimes they were necessary. Sometimes a patron needed a little grace. Maggie gave it whenever she could. But Arthur wasn't the sort to need reminders, nor was he the sort to forget to return a book.

She pulled up the staff log. The manual adjustment had been made yesterday afternoon, after the body had already been found and removed, and after most of the town had been told the same comforting story.

The staff member listed wasn't Maggie. It wasn't anyone she'd rostered on.

Maggie stared at the screen, her pulse quickening now, not with fear but with a sharp, clean certainty. Someone had been in the system. Someone had accessed Arthur's borrowing record after his death. Someone had decided that a book linked to council minutes needed to be kept quiet, or at least blurred enough to avoid standing out.

Maggie quietly printed the borrowing summaryand slid the page into a folder she labelled with Arthur's name. She didn't make it look secretive. She didn't hide it under stacks. She placed it where she could reach it again.

Then she did one more thing.

She logged in to the catalogue and searched for the council minutes volume. The system showed it as checked out to Arthur. Maggie clicked through and noted the exact reference number, the year range, and the shelf location it would have been in. She wrote down the lot numbers referenced in Arthur's notes that sat near the missing pages, keeping her handwriting small and neat.

When she closed the notebook and switched off her desk lamp, the library had already emptied. Late-afternoon light angled through the window, catching dust in the air. Outside, life in town continued as usual.

Maggie locked the library and walked home with the folder in her bag, lost in thought.

Martin was in the kitchen when she arrived, hands wet at the sink, turning to look at her immediately.

'How was today?' he asked.

Maggie hung her coat and set her bag down. 'People are already repeating the same story.'

He dried his hands. 'What story?'

'That it wasn't suspicious,' Maggie said. 'That it was a medical episode. That it's sad but simple.'

Martin's face softened. 'And you don't

believe it.'

'No,' Maggie replied. She took the folder from her bag and held it out, not dramatically, simply. 'Someone accessed his library record after he died.'

Martin took the folder and opened it, scanning the page. 'What am I looking at?'

'A council minutes volume Arthur borrowed,' Maggie said. 'It hasn't been returned. The due date was adjusted yesterday, and it wasn't done by me.'

Martin looked up slowly. 'Could it be a mistake?'

'It could,' Maggie said. 'But I don't think so.'

Martin's mouth tightened. 'So, what are you going to do?'

Maggie didn't answer immediately. She watched him, the steady practicality of him, the concern in his eyes. She didn't want to frighten him. She felt alive. She wasn't frightened. She was clear.

'I'm going to find out who changed it,' she said. 'And why.'

Martin held her gaze. 'Be careful, Maggie.'

'I will,' she said, and meant it. Then she added, quieter, 'But I can't leave this.'

That night, Maggie lay in bed, listening to Martin's breathing slow beside her as he drifted off to sleep. Maggie's mind, however, stayed alert, moving through facts rather than feelings.

Arthur had been careful. Arthur had been asking questions. Arthur had written down those initials twice, as if they mattered. His pages had been removed. His library record had been altered after his death.

The town wanted closure. The police wanted routine. People wanted reassurance, but Maggie wanted the truth.

Chapter Eight

The following morning, Maggie noticed how certain everyone sounded. It wasn't that people suddenly knew more than they had the day before; it was that they no longer felt the need to question anything. By the time Maggie unlocked the library doors, the explanation for Arthur Bell's death had settled into place, repeated often enough to feel complete, even though very little of it had actually been confirmed. The words varied slightly from person to person, but the meaning stayed the same, delivered with the kind of reassurance people preferred when they wanted a difficult thing to be finished with.

She heard it as she lifted the blinds and switched on the lights, scanning returns and answering questions about due dates and computer bookings. Arthur's name was spoken softly and respectfully, followed by a conclusion that seemed to close the subject every time.

'He must have been out walking.'

'They said it was his heart.'

'With the ground the way it was, he probably slipped.'

'At least it wasn't anything worse.'

Maggie listened without correcting anyone, though she found herself paying attention to what wasn't being said. No one mentioned whether Arthur had planned to walk or drive that morning. No one said they had seen his car or noted where it usually parked at that time of day. The assumption that he had been on foot slipped easily into place, accepted without anyone stopping to check whether it actually fitted.

By mid-morning, Maggie noticed how often habit was mistaken for certainty. Arthur was described as predictable, with his movements assumed to follow the same pattern each day, even by people who admitted they hadn't seen him at all that morning. Someone mentioned his usual café time; another spoke of his walks along the river. But when Maggie gently asked whether they had actually seen him, their answers softened and grew less sure.

'I thought I might have,' one woman said after a pause. 'But it could've been someone else. It was drizzling.'

Another person said they'd noticed a figure near the path earlier than usual but couldn't say which way the person was heading. No one mentioned a car parked where it didn't belong, or one that should have been there but wasn't. Maggie began to realise that the assumption of walking solved more problems than it created.

Arthur was a man of habits, but habits don't equate to strict schedules. Maggie understood this better than most. Many people mistake routine for exactness, assuming that if someone usually behaves a certain way, they always will. Arthur never seemed rigid to her; curious individuals rarely were.

Later that morning, Maggie reviewed the notices that had come through from the council and the police liaison. The language was careful and reassuring. The death was being treated as non-suspicious. The post-mortem was routine. No further action was anticipated. There were no times listed, no reference to how Arthur had travelled that morning, and no mention of whether his car had been considered relevant.

She read the wording twice, then a third time, before closing the email. It struck her that once the idea of walking had been accepted, the car simply disappeared from the story. It no longer needed to be accounted for.

Around lunchtime, Maggie watched the street from the window as people went about their day. Cars entered and exited parking spots, doors opened and shut, and engines revved and died down. The scene was steady, typical, and unremarkable. She caught herself thinking about Arthur's car, not because she thought it was missing or unusual, but because no one appeared to notice it at all.

If Arthur had planned to walk, the car should have been at home. If he intended to drive somewhere initially and walk later, the car would be elsewhere. In either case, this revealed his intent, which was important. No one had thought to verify this. It seemed like a lapse on the police's part, or perhaps something more— could it be a cover-up?

That afternoon, the head injury was

brought up again, casually mentioned as if it were merely an afterthought rather than something significant. Someone suggested he probably hit his head during the fall, while another claimed they'd heard he struck a rock near the path. The origin of this detail was unclear, and it had seamlessly merged into the broader explanation without any apparent dispute. Maggie observed that the injury was consistently described as a result rather than a cause. It was associated with the fall in people's perceptions, fitting neatly into the heart-attack story. No one seemed to consider that it might warrant independent scrutiny.

That afternoon, a man Maggie recognised as one of Arthur's occasional walking companions came into the library to return a book. She processed it and mentioned Arthur in passing, keeping her tone neutral.

'You must miss him on the path,' she said.

'Yes,' he replied. 'Though we didn't always walk together. Depends on the day.'

'What time did you usually head out?' Maggie asked.

He hesitated. 'It varied. Arthur liked to take his time.'

'Did you see him that morning?'

The man shook his head slowly. 'No. I thought I might have at first, but the more I think about it, the less sure I am.'

Maggie nodded silently. The uncertainty felt more genuine than the confident assumptions she'd been hearing all day.

As the afternoon progressed, Maggie went back to the systems she trusted most. She carefully reverified access permissions, not because she anticipated an obvious issue, but because patterns often emerge through repetition. The list of individuals authorised to make after-hours changes stayed small—so small that access itself was significant. She did not jump to conclusions; instead, she observed roles, subtle authority, and how permissions were granted and seldom revisited.

Later, Maggie sat at her desk and carefully started to piece together Arthur's morning from her notes. He was not at the café, and no one knew exactly when he left home. It was also unclear whether he intended to walk or drive. Since it was assumed he was walking, there was no need to consider his car or question his intentions.

What unsettled her was the unexplored span of time—a quiet morning window where Arthur's actions were only guessed at, not understood. It was lengthy enough for something else to occur and for the story to become significant.

Before leaving for the day, Maggie logged into the catalogue again and subtly marked the council minutes volume that Arthur had borrowed. It was a minor action, easily missed, but it allowed her to be notified if anything regarding the record was modified. She also did the same with Arthur's account, not making any changes, just making sure she would be aware if someone else made any updates.

When she locked the library and stepped outside, the town carried on as usual. People greeted each other, and a laugh rang out from outside the café. Cars drove by, their movement unremarkable, each one heading to a destination.

Maggie headed home, hoping the walk and fresh air would calm her mind.

Chapter Nine

Maggie set out that morning without a specific plan, only a general direction. She had a rare half-day off.

The river was a constant in her days in Wattle River- familiar enough to be comfortable but rarely drawing her attention. She crossed it daily on her way into town, saw glimpses of it between the buildings, and heard it mentioned in casual conversations whenever the weather changed. She didn't usually think of the river as holding answers. However, recently she realised how often people used it as a way to avoid facing difficult truths directly.

If something went missing, the river was the solution. If it wasn't found immediately, the river was blamed. It carried things away, took them, and made questions more difficult.

That morning, instead of heading straight home, Maggie turned towards the path that ran alongside the water and followed it upstream.

The air remained cool, and the ground felt firmer beneath her feet after the rain stopped. The river flowed steadily nearby, neither rushing nor stagnant, its surface occasionally disrupted by fallen branches and swirling where the current was impeded. Maggie walked at a leisurely pace, her focus shifting between her observations and the assumptions others might have.

Arthur Bell was supposed to have been walking here. That was the story everyone accepted. He went out, took his usual route, experienced a medical episode, and fell. The river was only seen as scenery in this version, serving as a backdrop to an unfortunate but unremarkable event.

What nobody appeared to consider was why he would have decided to walk that route in the first place.

Maggie was familiar with Arthur's routines and understood that his walks served a purpose. He preferred knowing his destination and the reason for his walk. Sometimes that meant taking a lengthy route, while on other days he paused to observe something that had previously piqued his interest. He wasn't inflexible, but he was attentive and deliberate. And he wasn't someone who left decisions to chance.

As Maggie moved further upstream, the housing became less frequent, and the path narrowed. Access points appeared and vanished—some clearly visible, others partially hidden by shrubs and overgrowth. She observed them silently, memorising their locations. There were spots where a car could discreetly pull off, and gentle slopes that made approaching the water easier without attracting attention. None of it appeared suspicious by itself. That wasn't the main issue. The point was that if someone wanted privacy, the river offered it.

Maggie paused at the bend in the path and looked back at the town. The traffic noise was quieter here, muted by distance and the gentle sound of flowing water. It occurred to her that people naturally think of things going downstream, things drifting away.

She hadn't encountered anyone mentioning upstream so far. Not once. All assumptions and casual comments pointed to the same idea: if something entered the river, it would flow away from the town, not toward it. This conclusion was simple to make and just as easy to ignore.

Maggie turned back and continued walking.

She navigated a section where the bank was steeper and the water darker, moving with a gentle yet powerful current that made judging its depth difficult. Her mind returned to Arthur's head injury, recalling how it was quickly mentioned and then dismissed, as if it were just an accident—a fall, a knock, a regrettable outcome of a medical incident.

It was a neat explanation, but it relied on a particular order of events. Heart attack first. Fall second. Injury last.

No one had said how that order had been confirmed.

She slowed near a place where the path dipped slightly, and the ground showed signs of recent disturbance, subtle enough not to attract notice but enough to indicate occasional passage. Perhaps fishermen, walkers, or someone taking a shortcut.

She didn't pause for long because there

was no need. She wasn't searching for anything particular at the moment. Instead, she allowed the place to speak in its own way, helping her understand what was possible rather than what was expected.

On her return journey to town, Maggie saw an older man by the water with a fishing rod. He nodded as she went by and then spoke.

'River's been carrying a bit lately,' he said. 'After the rain.'

'Yes,' Maggie replied. 'It always does.'

'People lose things in there all the time,' he continued. 'Once it takes hold, that's it. You won't see it again.'

Maggie smiled politely. 'Depends where it goes, I suppose.'

The man laughed. 'Downstream, usually. That's the way of it.'

Maggie continued walking, the comment lingering in her thoughts. Usually, it was about downstream. Such statements were often accepted without question because they seem true enough. However, rivers don't only flow in a single direction. They eddy, loop, and trap objects unexpectedly. Likewise, people can also influence things if they decide to.

Back in town, Maggie took the long way home, passing Arthur's street without slowing. His house sat quietly, unchanged, the garden beginning to look untended at the edges. No car sat out front. That absence had become normal far too quickly.

She wondered who had last seen it. Not in passing, not as an afterthought, but properly noticed it.

At home, Maggie prepared tea and sat at the kitchen table with her notebook. She didn't start writing right away; instead, she replayed her walk in her mind—recalling the sensation of the ground beneath her feet, how the river narrowed and widened, and noting the areas where access was simple and where it was more difficult.

When she finally picked up her pen, she didn't list facts. She wrote questions.

Why walk and not drive?

Why that direction?

She reflected once more on the library record, the subtle change after Arthur's death, and the council email regarding routine reviews. She remembered Margaret Hill's composed confidence and how she emphasised timing and appropriateness over absolute truth.

Maggie leaned back in her chair, gazing out the window where the river was hidden but always nearby. She realised how useful the river was, often acting as an answer without any need for evidence. It transported objects. It wiped things away. It enabled people to move forward. But this only worked if one accepted the flow it was destined to take.

That evening, Martin asked how her walk had been.

'Good,' Maggie replied. 'Useful.'

He looked at her sceptically. 'That sounds ominous.'

She offered a gentle smile. 'Not ominous. Just clarifying.'

She didn't share more details yet. She wasn't prepared to fully articulate the story, not even for herself. She recognised enough to realise that the story everyone believed didn't quite match the world it was meant to belong to. Arthur Bell hadn't just vanished into his morning routine; something had shifted his day, changed his course, and rearranged the sequence of events. The river, despite its familiarity, had contributed to that shift, whether people acknowledged it or not.

Later, lying in bed, Maggie thought again

of the river upstream. It wasn't where people looked first. It required intention, effort, and a willingness to go against expectations. But if something had been placed there deliberately, it would stay hidden far longer than anything left to drift away.

The river had secrets, Maggie knew that now.

And so did the people who trusted it to keep them.

Chapter Ten

Maggie woke later than she did all week, the light already pressing gently against the curtains as if it had been waiting for permission to come in. The house felt different on a Saturday, softer at the edges, less insistent. There was no immediate sense of being behind, no mental list forming before she even sat up. She lay still for a moment, listening to the faint clatter from the kitchen and the low murmur of the radio, and let herself enjoy the unfamiliar luxury of not needing to move straight away.

Thoughts of Arthur appeared every morning since his death, but this time, they didn't tighten her chest. Instead, they lingered, present and unresolved, waiting. Maggie saw this change and considered it a small mercy.

When she finally got up, Martin was already dressed, standing at the bench with a mug of coffee in his hand and the paper spread open beside him. He glanced up as she came in, his expression softening into a ready smile.

'Morning,' she said as she leaned down to kiss him briefly.

'Morning, good sleep in?'

Maggie yawned. 'It was. I was so tired last night.'

They moved around each other with the comfort of long familiarity, neither feeling the need to fill the silence with words. Maggie was toasting bread while Martin read briefly from the newspaper, only mildly engaged, and stopped halfway when he noticed she wasn't truly paying attention. She offered him a small, apologetic smile, which he dismissed with a wave and a grin. He knew her well enough to know she was preoccupied with solving the death of Arthur – even if it wasn't supposed to be a mystery.

'You want to go for that walk later?' he asked, as if the idea had only just occurred to him.

'Yes,' Maggie said without hesitation. 'I think that would be good.'

They ate slowly, discussing everyday matters—such as a neighbour's excessively barking dog, the garden that would need care if the weather stayed nice, and a radio interview Martin had overheard earlier in the week. Suddenly, it felt important to allow these small things to fill the space, resisting the urge to let heavier thoughts overshadow every quiet moment.

After breakfast, Maggie cleared the table and wandered into the sitting room. The jigsaw puzzle sat on the low table near the window, exactly where she'd left it days earlier. It was a muted landscape, all soft greens and greys, the kind of image that revealed itself slowly rather than demanding attention. She sat down and tipped the open box toward her, letting the loose pieces slide into view.

She approached it calmly, never rushing. Instead, she started by sorting, loosely grouping similar colours, and separating edges from middles, letting her hands move freely without pressure. The steady rhythm kept her rooted in the present moment. She picked up a piece she had tried before, turned it a few times, then set it aside without frustration. Some pieces simply weren't ready yet; she had learned that long ago.

While working, her mind wandered in gentle loops, reflecting on the walk she and Martin had planned, and how people talked about the river as if it could solve problems by carrying them away. The assumption that if something was missing, it must have gone downstream. She fitted an edge piece into place and paused, her fingers lightly touching it. Moving upstream required more effort.

The idea came softly, not as a sudden insight, but as something that had finally taken form. She didn't push it further. Instead, she added one more piece, then another, until the image shifted subtly. Maggie relaxed, feeling content, and left the remaining work for later.

They left the house late in the morning, with the air cool but rapidly warming as the sun rose higher. The town had relaxed into its weekend pace, slower and more relaxed. Fewer cars travelled down the main street, and people took their time when they met, engaging in conversations without the usual looks at watches or phones.

They headed toward the river, their feet guided by routine. Maggie had nothing with her, no bag, no notebook, and she had also left her phone behind, a conscious decision. She preferred to let the day unfold without capturing it.

As they walked, the river flowed steadily beside them, its surface broken here and there by fallen branches and gentle swirls where water met resistance. Maggie realised how different it felt now—not because the river had changed, but because she had. Throughout the week, it had been a constant presence in her mind, whether she acknowledged it or not. Today, it simply existed as part of the landscape, no longer a question but a steady companion.

They passed familiar faces along the path. A woman walking her dog. A couple Maggie recognised from the café. There were nods and brief greetings, comments about the weather and how good it was to see the sun again.

Arthur's name didn't come up, and Maggie was aware of its absence even as she welcomed it.

Martin pointed out a pair of ducks drifting near the bank, their movement unhurried and loosely coordinated. Maggie watched them for a moment, smiling, before her attention drifted elsewhere. She found herself looking not at the water itself, but at the spaces around it. The bends in the path. The trees that offered cover. The places where the bank sloped gently enough to approach without difficulty.

'You're very quiet,' Martin said after a while.

'I'm enjoying it,' Maggie replied, and she meant it.

He nodded, accepting that easily, and they walked on in companionable silence. When they reached the point where the path split, one route looping back toward town and the other continuing upstream, Martin slowed.

'Want to keep going?' he asked.

Maggie looked ahead. The upstream path was narrower, less trafficked, but still well worn. She nodded. 'Yes.'

The sounds of town faded as they moved on, replaced by the steady hush of water and the soft crunch of gravel underfoot. The river felt different here, darker where shadows pooled, the current less visible but more insistent. Maggie noticed how the banks rose slightly, how the trees leaned closer, narrowing the view.

Martin kicked lightly at a stone, sending it skittering ahead. 'Funny how everyone assumes things end up downstream,' he said, not looking at her.

Maggie glanced at him. 'What do you mean?'

'You hear it all the time,' he said. 'If something's lost, people say the river took it. As if it only ever goes one way.'

'And you don't think it does?' Maggie asked.

He shrugged. 'Rivers do what they want. Depends on the current. The bends. What's underneath.' He smiled at her. 'Depends how well you know them.'

Maggie held his gaze for a moment, then looked back toward the water. The comment settled quietly in her mind. Filed away for later.

They went through a clearing where the ground was level by the bank, with grass flattened as if someone had recently paused there. Maggie saw it without stopping, noticing the detail and then continuing. There was no need to investigate further, and she didn't want to change the walk into something else.

A little further along, they passed a man fishing from a fallen log. He nodded at them as they went by.

'Good day for it,' he said.

'Yes,' Martin replied. 'Looks peaceful.'

The man gave a short laugh. 'Looks can be deceiving.'

Maggie glanced back once they'd passed, but the man had already turned his attention back to the water.

They walked until the path thinned further, the ground roughening beneath their feet. Martin slowed, reading Maggie's body language easily.

'This far enough?' he asked.

'Yes,' she said. 'Let's head back.'

On the return walk, Maggie felt lighter, as if a weight had eased but not completely disappeared. She no longer felt compelled to analyse every detail. Instead, she allowed the river to stay as it always had, wide and steady, carrying on without explanation.

Back near town, they stopped at a bench overlooking the water and sat for a while.

Martin stretched his legs out in front of him, leaning back on his hands.

'You've been carrying a lot,' he said quietly.

'I know,' Maggie replied.

'You don't have to work it all out at once.'

She smiled faintly. 'I'm not trying to.'

'But you are thinking.'

'Always.' She smiled.

He reached for her hand and squeezed it gently. 'Just remember, you don't have to do it alone.'

Maggie rested her hand in his and her head on his shoulder. She didn't answer straight away. She wasn't sure yet how much of what she was holding could be shared without placing him in the middle of something he hadn't asked for. But she appreciated the offer, the steadiness of him beside her. Her husband was a good man and she felt very lucky.

They walked home in the early afternoon, the town quieter now, as if everyone had agreed to take the day slowly. Maggie spent the rest of the afternoon doing ordinary things. Folding laundry. Watering the garden. Reading a few pages of a novel without absorbing much of it. The normality felt necessary, a reminder of what she was trying to protect as much as what she was trying to understand. She did a little more on the jigsaw puzzle too, pleased with her progress.

That evening, as the light dimmed, Maggie kept thinking about the walk. Not about any particular thing she saw, but about its overall shape. The upstream part felt intentional rather than random. Martin's remark about the river fit naturally, needing no explanation from either of them.

She slept better that night than she had in days.

Sunday unfolded much the same way. A slower breakfast. A shorter walk, looping back toward town rather than continuing upstream. Maggie noticed how naturally people spoke about the river when they passed it, as if it were a shared language everyone assumed they understood.

'That water'll hide anything,' a woman said to her companion as they crossed the bridge.

Maggie kept walking.

By late afternoon, the weight of the coming week began to settle back in. The library would open again tomorrow. The systems, the routines, the quiet expectations would return. Maggie felt ready for them in a way she hadn't been before.

That evening, she sat at the kitchen table with her notebook again. This time, she didn't write questions so much as shapes. She sketched the bend of the river as she knew it, marking access points from memory, not as evidence, but as understanding. She didn't label anything. She didn't draw conclusions. She simply recorded what she knew, and when she closed the notebook and set it aside, Maggie felt calm.

Arthur Bell hadn't vanished into the landscape. He'd moved through it, and someone else had moved through it as well. The river hadn't swallowed answers. It had merely been trusted to keep them.

Standing at the window, Maggie looked out toward where the river lay beyond the houses, unseen but present. The weekend had done what she'd needed it to do.

It had given her space to see clearly.

Chapter Eleven

By the time Maggie reached the library, she had already abandoned the idea that the day would be straightforward.

It wasn't so much instinct or premonition as a developing awareness that she was no longer navigating the story alone. Over the weekend, she sensed a change, she felt it even before opening the door, a feeling that the quiet she depended on had diminished, and that other hands were now involved in piecing together the puzzle she thought was hers alone.

Inside, the library was busier than usual earlier, though not crowded, but it felt unsettled. People moved purposefully instead of leisurely, frequently   glancing   around   rather   than browsing. Maggie observed this silently as she placed her bag under the desk and logged in. She bypassed notices and returns, knowing they could wait. Over the past week, she had learned to distinguish between routine tasks and urgent matters.

She started analysing the car first. She had contemplated the question so often that it no longer seemed hypothetical, but rather practical. Arthur Bell did not always walk; he drove when it was convenient, and no one could provide a clear or consistent answer about its current location. The missing car had been seamlessly integrated into the overall story of his death, as if once it was ruled non-suspicious, all other details associated with it were automatically dismissed. Maggie had spent too long working with systems to accept that as accidental.

She waited until the counter cleared, then picked up the phone and dialled Senior

Constable Harris. The call connected quickly.

'Maggie Ellis,' she said. 'From the library.'

'Yes,' Harris replied. His voice was professional, neutral. 'How can I help you?'

'I'm following up on something small,' Maggie said. 'Arthur Bell's vehicle. Has it been located?'

There was a pause, slight but unmistakable.

'It's been dealt with,' Harris said.

Maggie closed her eyes briefly. 'I'm not sure I've heard that it was found.'

'At this stage,' Harris said carefully, 'it's not considered relevant.'

'Because you've determined the death was non-suspicious,' Maggie said.

'That's correct.'

'So there's no active effort to locate it.'

Another pause. Longer this time.

'It's been noted,' Harris said. 'If it becomes relevant, we'll revisit it.'

Maggie felt something settle into place. Not anger. Not shock. Recognition.

'Can you tell me who logged that decision?' she asked.

'I'm not sure that's information I can provide,' Harris replied.

'All right,' Maggie said. 'Thank you for clarifying.'

She hung up before he could offer reassurance she didn't want to hear.

She paused briefly, hands folded, as she reflected on the conversation. What mattered more was the form of the words rather than their content. The initial assumption had been established early, shaping everything that followed. The car was not lost; it was just rendered irrelevant.

She returned to the computer and opened

the internal catalogue, navigating swiftly now, without the hesitation she might have shown a week earlier. Arthur's borrowing history remained the same. The missing council minutes volume was still present, its due date silently updated, and its status unremarkable unless you understood what you were looking at.

Maggie clicked into the staff access log again and scanned the entries more carefully this time. Her jaw tightened. The adjustment had been made late in the afternoon on the day Arthur's body was removed. After she'd gone home. After most of the town had been told there was nothing to worry about. And it hadn't been made by anyone currently rostered. That didn't mean she knew who had done it. But it did mean she knew who hadn't.

She printed the log, folded the page once, and tucked it into her bag without marking it.

She avoided looking around as she did it, knowing there was no need. If she was being watched now, subtlety was more important than secrecy.

A voice cut across her thoughts.

'Maggie?'

She looked up to see Len standing at the counter, his expression curious, a little too alert for a casual visit.

'Everything all right?' he asked.

'Yes,' Maggie responded. After a brief pause, she asked, 'Why do you ask?'

Len shrugged. 'Just seems busy today.'

'It is,' Maggie agreed.

He lingered, shifting his weight. 'You hear anything more from the police?'

'Nothing new,' Maggie said. 'Same as before.'

Len nodded, apparently satisfied, but he didn't leave straight away. His eyes drifted toward the workroom door behind her, then back again.

'They'll let you know if anything changes,' he said. 'Best not to get ahead of things.'

Maggie smiled politely. 'I'm not.'

Len left, but the sense of being observed remained.

She waited until the desk was quiet again, then rose and moved toward the back room. That's where the local history materials were stored, organised and catalogued, typically untouched unless someone knew precisely what they needed. Maggie thought she could take her time going through them.

She was wrong.

The shelf where the council minutes volumes were usually kept was half empty.

Maggie paused, her heart pounding briefly. She stepped closer, examining the remaining book spines. She noticed two volumes were missing. Not just the one Arthur had borrowed.

She slowly turned and surveyed the room. Everything seemed untouched, with no boxes out of place, no sign of a hasty escape. This wasn't a spontaneous theft; it was a calculated, deliberate act.

Margaret Hill's words from earlier in the week came back to her. A review. Early days. Nothing major.

Maggie reached for the catalogue terminal and searched for the missing volumes. One was marked 'in use'. The other had been reclassified as 'temporarily unavailable'. She stared at the screen, then closed it.

This was no longer a coincidence. Someone had decided those records should not be easily accessed, and they had done it quietly, with enough authority that no one else thought to question it.

Footsteps sounded in the corridor behind her.

'Maggie.'

She turned to find Margaret herself standing in the doorway, handbag hooked over her arm, her expression composed.

'I thought I might find you back here,' Margaret said.

'Did you?' Maggie replied.

Margaret smiled. 'You've always been thorough.'

Maggie gestured toward the shelf. 'You know those volumes have been removed.'

'Yes,' Margaret said easily. 'As part of the review.'

'Which review?' Maggie asked.

Margaret tilted her head. 'You're asking a lot of questions for someone who works in a library.'

Maggie held her gaze. 'Libraries exist

because people ask questions.'

Margaret's smile thinned. 'People also expect stability.'

'Not at the cost of accuracy,' Maggie said.

Margaret stepped closer, lowering her voice. 'I'd hate for you to misunderstand what's happening here. No one is accusing you of anything. But it would be unfortunate if your role became… complicated.'

Maggie experienced its weight at that moment. It was not a threat, but a recalibration.

'I'm doing my job,' she said.

Margaret nodded. 'Just be careful which parts of it you prioritise.'

When Margaret left, Maggie didn't follow. She waited until the sound of her footsteps faded, then reached into her bag and pulled out the folded log page again. She studied it briefly, then tucked it into a different folder, one she hadn't used in years. She was no longer invisible. And she was no longer willing to pretend that mattered less than it did.

Maggie didn't return to the front desk straight away. She stayed in the back room long enough to let the library fall into its own rhythm without her. Voices rose and fell beyond the door, the soft clatter of returned books and the low murmur of conversation filtering through. Normally, that sound grounded her. Today, it felt like a cover. Like the town continuing its life while something else happened just beneath the surface.

She crossed to the worktable and opened the folder she'd brought from home. Inside were copies of Arthur's borrowing history, her handwritten notes, and the printed staff log. She spread them out carefully, aligning the edges, the way she did with jigsaw pieces before starting. She wasn't looking for the whole picture yet. She was looking for corners.

The missing council minutes volumes formed one corner. The altered borrowing record formed another. And then there was the car. Still unlocated. Still dismissed as irrelevant. That was the gap.

She stood, closed the folder, and slid it back into her bag. Waiting would only make things easier for the people who preferred her to wait. If access was being restricted, she needed to move while she still could.

At the front desk, Maureen was returning a stack of books, her mouth set in a thin line. 'You look busy,' she said.

'I am,' Maggie replied.

Maureen hesitated, then leaned closer. 'Margaret's been around this morning.'

Maureen glanced toward the back room, then lowered her voice. 'She's been asking questions.'

'So have I,' Maggie said.

Maureen gave a small, nervous laugh. 'That's not always the same thing.'

Maggie met her gaze. 'Did Arthur ever mention where he went when he wanted to think?'

Maureen blinked. 'That's a strange question.'

'He didn't like being interrupted,' Maggie said. 'If he was working through something, he wouldn't stay at home.'

Maureen's eyes flicked toward the window, then back. 'He used to park near the old access track. Up past the bend. Said it was quiet.'

'Did he walk from there?'

'Sometimes.' Maureen hesitated. 'Sometimes he just sat in the car.'

Maggie nodded. 'Thank you.'

Maureen straightened, gathering her books. 'Be careful,' she said softly, then left without waiting for a response.

Maggie didn't waste the moment. She closed the library for lunch without fanfare, locking the front door and pinning the sign in place with a steadiness she didn't entirely feel. She didn't go home for lunch. Martin was at the Men's Shed today anyway. She hurried back home, grabbed the keys and headed straight for her car.

The access track Maureen had mentioned wasn't officially marked anymore. It had once been used by council vehicles and anglers, back when the river was more accessible in that stretch. Now it existed in a sort of administrative limbo. Not closed, exactly. Just not encouraged.

Maggie parked well back from the track and walked the rest of the way, the ground uneven beneath her feet. She wasn't expecting to find Arthur's car. Not really. If it were that simple, it wouldn't have been overlooked. What she was looking for was evidence of attention. Tyre marks. Disturbed ground. The sense that someone else had been there recently.

The track curved gently before dropping toward the riverbank. Maggie slowed, scanning the ground. There were indications of recent activity, but nothing specific she could confirm as significant. Still, she took a few photos, not necessarily to prove anything now, but in case they might be useful later.

She stood for a moment at the edge, letting the scene set in her mind. This was where Arthur had come when he needed space. Where he could think without interruption. Where he could park without being seen.

And where something had gone wrong.

A sound behind her made her turn sharply.

A man stood several metres away, hands in his pockets, his expression unreadable. She recognised him after a moment. One of the council maintenance workers. Not someone she knew well, but familiar enough to place.

'Didn't expect to see anyone out here,' he said.

'I could say the same,' Maggie replied.

He shrugged. 'Just checking the track. There's talk it might be closed off.'

'Why?'

He hesitated. 'Safety.'

'Because of Arthur?' Maggie asked.

His jaw tightened. 'That's not what I meant.'

Maggie studied him. 'Has anyone asked you to check this area recently?'

He shifted his weight. 'I've been told to make notes. That's all.'

'By whom?'

He shook his head. 'I'm not getting involved.'

'You already are,' Maggie said gently.

He looked at her for a long moment, then exhaled. 'Someone came through here late last week. Not council. I thought it was odd.'

'Did you report it?'

He nodded. 'To my supervisor.'

'And?'

'And I was told it wasn't relevant.'

Maggie felt the now-familiar click of recognition. 'Thank you.'

He left without another word.

Maggie lingered a bit longer before turning back. She didn't feel triumphant but rather confirmed in her feelings. It was the sense that she was confronting something tangible, structured, and that preferred its decisions not questioned.

Back at the library, she unlocked the door and stepped inside. She went to the catalogue terminal and logged in under her credentials. She had access to more than people realised. Not because she abused it, but because she knew how systems were built. She searched for the council minutes volumes again. One had been fully removed from public view. The other had been assigned a placeholder status, as though it had never existed. Maggie didn't hesitate. She pulled the physical inventory records, printed what she could, and scanned the remainder to a secure drive. She wasn't stealing. She was preserving.

A shadow crossed the doorway.

'Maggie.'

Len again.

'You shouldn't be here,' he said. 'Library's closed.'

'I reopened,' Maggie replied. 'Briefly.'

He frowned. 'That's not how this is meant to go.'

She looked at him steadily. 'Who told you that?'

He hesitated, then laughed, short and humourless. 'You always did ask the wrong questions.'

Maggie closed the folder she'd been working on. 'Arthur asked the same ones.'

Len's face hardened. 'Arthur went too far.'

'Or someone else did,' Maggie said.

Silence stretched between them.

'You're making things difficult,' Len said finally.

'Good,' Maggie replied.

He left without another word.

Maggie released the breath she'd been holding. That was definitely a threat. But why? What did Len have to hide?

Maggie finished what she was doing, then logged out and shut the terminal down properly. She placed the drive in her bag and locked the cabinet where the remaining records sat. It wouldn't stop anyone determined, but it would slow them down.

That night, she spread the copied records out on the dining table, sliding them into place the way she did with jigsaw pieces, turning them until the edges aligned. Martin watched her quietly from the kitchen.

'You're sure?' he asked.

'Yes,' Maggie said. 'They're closing ranks.'

'And the car?'

'Still missing,' Maggie replied. 'And I don't think it's because they haven't found it.'

Martin leaned against the doorway. 'Be careful.'

'I am,' she said. 'But I'm not stopping.'

Later, when the house was quiet, Maggie sat with a jigsaw on the table, the pieces spread before her. She fitted one into place, then another, working one piece at a time. She wasn't trying to rush the picture. The image was emerging now. Not complete, not yet, but enough that she could see where the gaps were. Enough to know that something had been deliberately misplaced.

And someone was counting on her not noticing.

She smiled faintly and reached for the next piece.

Chapter Twelve

Maggie had been at the library less than fifteen minutes when June Wallace walked in with her phone held out like proof.

'They've blocked it,' June said, voice clipped. 'The file Arthur was helping me with. It was there one day and gone the next.'

Maggie didn't take the phone straight away. She looked at June first, at the set of her mouth and the way she held her shoulders, tense and lifted, as if bracing herself. June wasn't prone to fuss. If she was upset about something, there was likely a good reason.

'Show me,' Maggie said.

June unlocked the screen and tapped through. A council portal page loaded, then redirected to a bland notice about a temporary review. No contact name. No explanation beyond a single sentence requesting patience.

Maggie nodded once. 'Did you receive an email?'

'No,' June snapped. 'If I hadn't checked, I'd never have known. Which is exactly the point.'

Maggie logged in to her terminal, maintaining a calm, steady pace. She scanned the catalogue entries Arthur had been reviewing, now familiar to her. The public view showed the same soft lock June had encountered, a polite obstacle, a closed door that seemed temporary. She clicked into the backend view available only to staff. The files were still there, intact and complete, quietly redirected from public access.

'They've masked it,' Maggie said. 'Not deleted it.'

June's eyebrows lifted. 'So someone's flicked a switch.'

'Yes.'

June leaned closer. 'Arthur said the boundary didn't make sense. He said it looked like someone shifted it quietly, on paper, and then behaved as if it had always been that way.'

Maggie opened the access log. The timestamp confirmed what she already suspected. The restriction had been applied early that morning, before most people would have been checking. Efficient. Deliberate.

'Does it say who did it?' June asked.

'It says a council administrator credential was used,' Maggie replied. She didn't add that the credential was broad enough to cover several people. 'If anyone contacts you directly about this, let me know.'

June hesitated. 'Are you sure you want to get involved?'

Maggie met her gaze. 'I already am.'

June nodded once and left.

Maggie had barely returned to shelving when the printer behind the desk began feeding pages she hadn't sent. It was an old machine, prone to quirks, but it had never printed on its own.

She crossed quickly and grabbed the last page before it slipped onto the tray. It bore council letterhead, a dated reference number, and language that avoided direct meaning while suggesting urgency. She gathered the pages and scanned them. They weren't explosive, but they were revealing. References to access tracks, risk management, time sensitivity, and movement along the riverbank, framed as maintenance rather than scrutiny.

Someone had routed a job through the wrong terminal.

Maggie slid the pages into a plain manila

folder and tucked it under the counter. She didn't stand there reading or invite unwanted attention.

A mother and child stepped up to the desk to return picture books. Maggie helped them, recommended another series, and handed the child a sticker. The library continued to function, exactly as it needed to. In a place built on order, any disruption was instantly noticeable.

By late morning, two additional patrons inquired about restricted local records. They did so calmly, without anger or raising their voices, but their questions were made close together. One was a man who hovered among others' research without engaging in much of his own. The other was an older woman Maggie had not previously seen, interested in council minutes. Maggie gave both the same answer and watched them leave. One glanced back through the glass as if checking whether Maggie was watching.

At eleven, she ran the children's reading session, but her heart wasn't in it today. She had too much on her mind. Five children sat cross-legged on the mat while two parents hovered nearby. Maggie read steadily, pointed the book at the right moments, and asked simple questions. For ten minutes, the room was loud and uncomplicated.

When Rhyme Time was over, Maggie returned the book to the desk and carried on.

Senior Constable Harris arrived just after midday. He came straight to the desk, voice low. 'Maggie.'

'Senior Constable Harris,' she replied.

'We need to talk.'

'If it's off the record, you can speak here,' Maggie said. 'If it's not, email me.'

Harris's jaw tightened. 'People have made complaints.'

'About what?'

'About you encouraging speculation.'

Maggie scanned another return. 'People speculate without encouragement.'

'You've been accessing records you don't need.'

'Everything I access is within my role.'

'Not if it's personal.'

Maggie stopped scanning and looked at him. 'Arthur Bell's file was altered after his death. That isn't personal. That's procedural.'

Harris's eyes flicked, just once. 'It was likely an administrative correction.'

'It wasn't,' Maggie said. 'Because it wasn't necessary, and it wasn't done by any rostered staff.'

'We're not treating this as suspicious.'

'And the missing car?' Maggie asked.

Harris's mouth tightened. 'We've been over that.'

'No,' Maggie said. 'You've avoided it.'

'We'll locate it if it becomes relevant.'

'It's relevant now.'

Harris leaned closer. 'You're stepping outside your lane. Leave the police work to the police.'

'Then please do your job and investigate this properly,' Maggie said.

He left without any further comment, and Maggie knew she'd hit a nerve.

At lunch, Maggie stayed open. She worked through the backend logs again, this time tracking patterns rather than files. Access tags were being applied in clusters, masking one trail while leaving others untouched. Someone was being selective.

At one-thirty, Margaret Hill arrived and wasted no time on pleasantries.

'This has gone far enough,' Margaret said.

Maggie gestured toward the table near the

reference shelves. 'Would you like to take a seat?' Margaret remained standing.

'You're making people uneasy.'

'Arthur is dead,' Maggie replied. 'People should be uneasy.'

'You're not the police.'

'No,' Maggie said. 'Which is why I'm asking why the police aren't acting like police.'

Margaret leaned forward. 'You don't understand the damage you could cause.'

'To whom?' Maggie asked.

Margaret's gaze flicked away for a fraction, then returned. Maggie noticed.

Margaret stood. 'You're out of your depth. You need to back off before something else happens.'

Margaret left, and Maggie had a feeling that Margaret had been sent to deliver this message. But by whom?

Maggie kept working until closing time,

then locked the office door and retrieved the last council volume from the cabinet. She examined it as Arthur would have: skimming for particular terms, noting meeting dates, and tracking adjustments related to land near the river and the access track. Everything seemed organised on paper, perhaps too organised. She scanned the relevant pages and placed the book in a plain storage box under her desk.

After closing, she went home, ate quickly with Martin, and suggested a walk. He agreed without hesitation. He had a feeling there was more to this walk, and he didn't want her to go alone.

They drove to the access track and parked where the verge widened. Maggie paused, scanning the road, then nodded. The track had been used again. Not just tyre marks, but scuffed ground where someone had walked back and forth.

'This wasn't here yesterday,' Martin said.

'No,' Maggie replied.

They followed the track down toward the bend, keeping their distance from the water. The river flowed steadily, its dark surface obscuring depth and movement below. Maggie concentrated on the bank, especially the shallow slope where tyres could dangerously get too close. She photographed the area, including landmarks, then zoomed toward a darker patch where the current shifted.

'Something's there,' Martin said.

'Or was,' Maggie replied.

An engine sounded above them.

They turned together as a council vehicle pulled in. A man stepped out, supervisor by the look of him, boots barely marked.

'You shouldn't be down here,' he called.

'This isn't closed,' Maggie said.

'It will be. We're assessing risk.'

'Risk? What risk?'

'People slipping.'

Maggie nodded. 'Funny that hasn't come up before.'

'You need to leave.'

'You've been here already,' Maggie said. 'And not just today.'

He hesitated, then Maggie pressed on. 'Why hasn't this area been officially closed? Why move quietly instead of following proper procedures?'

'That's not my call.'

'But you're carrying it out.'

His gaze flicked toward the river before he could stop himself.

'You're worried what people might see,' Maggie said.

'You don't know what you're talking about.'

'I know you don't want me here,' Maggie

replied.

He left without another word.

Maggie took one final photograph before they walked back to the car.

Later, at home, Maggie backed up the scans and placed the folder from the printer job into a plain drawer. The town fell into its familiar quietness with just the sounds of the night. An owl hooted, and cows lowed in the distance.

Maggie sat at the dining table with a cup of tea. Someone was trying to keep the riverbank quiet. Someone was tightening access. Someone was smoothing Arthur Bell's work as if he'd never been close to anything that mattered.

Maggie confirmed that Martin had locked the door before she walked down the hall to join him in bed. His snores could already be heard from the bedroom, and she found him fast asleep, with his book face down beside him.

Tomorrow, she would go back to the library, open it as she always did, and during the gaps between patrons, she would continue tugging at the only remaining threads that still moved.

Chapter Thirteen

Maggie had just finished reshelving a trolley of returns when Maureen slipped back into the library, moving with the determined purpose of someone who did not intend to browse. Maureen didn't continue all the way to the desk this time. She stopped halfway down the aisle and caught Maggie's eye, lifting her chin once in a way that was unmistakably a summons.

Maggie hesitated only long enough to check that the front desk was covered, then followed her between the shelves.

'They've been up near the old access track,' Maureen said quietly, not bothering with preamble. 'Two council vehicles. Not maintenance, not utilities. Council.'

Maggie felt the words settle rather than land. 'How do you know?'

'My nephew was driving past on his way to Scone. He rang me because he knows I keep an eye on these things.' Maureen's mouth tightened. 'They weren't fixing anything. They were standing around looking at the river.'

Maggie nodded. 'Did he recognise anyone?'

'One of them, yes. A bloke who's done odd jobs for council for years. Never seen him near that track before.'

Maggie glanced instinctively toward the front windows, though the river itself wasn't visible from here. 'Did they say why they were there?'

Maureen gave a short, humourless laugh. 'Council never says why, so he didn't bother asking.'

Maggie thanked her and watched her go, a

familiar feeling of gratitude mixed with something more pointed. Information was spreading, albeit informally and somewhat haphazardly, but she had captured people's attention. The right people were listening, while others were attempting to deter her curiosity.

Back at her desk, Maggie attempted to focus on her work, but the tone of the day had shifted. The library activity fluctuated as visitors came and went in waves. Books were borrowed, returned, and inquired about.

A man Maggie knew only by sight lingered longer than necessary at the counter. 'Strange business,' he said, nodding vaguely. 'But I suppose these things happen.'

Maggie only responded with a polite murmur, understanding that silence often implied agreement and felt safer.

Once the rush slowed down, she quietly moved into the back office and shut the door.

The folder labelled with Arthur's name was left exactly where she had placed it, intentionally left in plain sight rather than concealed. Maggie picked it up, laid it on the desk, and opened it.

She reviewed the printed borrowing summary once more, even though she knew it by heart. She checked the changed return date, the missing council minutes volume, and the staff log entry that didn't belong to anyone on duty. She opened the catalogue, bringing up the record again to verify the reference numbers she had noted the previous night. The sequence was important. If Arthur had been working through the records methodically, the gap revealed its own story. He had been close to something when the pages were removed.

A soft knock sounded at the door.

Maggie closed the folder and turned. 'Yes?'

Helen Carter stepped inside, takeaway

coffee in her hand, her expression caught somewhere between concern and irritation. 'I thought I'd find you back here.'

'What's wrong?' Maggie asked.

Helen folded her arms. 'There's a man out the front asking questions. Not the police. Says he's from the council. The new girl looks a bit flustered.'

Maggie felt a familiar tightening behind her ribs. 'What sort of questions?'

'He wants to know whether Arthur used the public computers here. And whether you keep records of that.'

Maggie stood. 'Did she answer him?'

Helen shook her head. 'She told him to speak to you.'

'Good,' Maggie said. 'I'll handle it.'

The man was waiting near the noticeboard, tall, clean-shaven, holding himself with the confidence of someone used to access. He turned when Maggie approached, offering a polite smile that didn't quite reach his eyes.

'Maggie Ellis?' he asked.

'Yes.'

'I'm Tom Ridley,' he said. 'Wattle River Council. I was hoping to ask a few questions.'

Maggie gestured toward the desk. 'About Arthur Bell?'

Ridley nodded. 'Yes. Specifically, his use of library resources.'

'What about them?'

Ridley glanced around, as though gauging how much of the conversation might travel. 'Council's doing a routine review of records access. We just want to be clear about what materials were available and whether any assistance was given.'

Maggie kept her voice level. 'Arthur accessed public materials. The same ones available to anyone.'

'Of course,' Ridley said. 'But he did have a particular interest in council minutes, didn't he?'

'He had an interest in local history,' Maggie replied. 'That's not unusual.'

Ridley smiled again. 'No, I suppose not.'

Maggie met his gaze. 'If the council has concerns about Arthur's research, you're welcome to put them in writing.'

'That won't be necessary,' Ridley said quickly. 'We're simply closing off loose ends.'

Maggie nodded. 'Then I'm sure you won't mind me asking why council vehicles were at the old access track this morning.'

The pause was brief, but it was there. Ridley's smile thinned. 'Routine inspection. Erosion concerns.'

'Interesting,' Maggie said. 'Given that section of the bank was stabilised only a few years ago.'

Ridley shifted his weight. 'Conditions change.'

'Yes, they do. So do stories,' Maggie said calmly.

Ridley straightened. 'If you recall anything else about Arthur's activities, I'd appreciate a call.'

'I'll let the police know,' Maggie replied.

Ridley inclined his head and left, his footsteps brisk, purposeful.

Helen appeared beside Maggie. 'He didn't like that.'

'No,' Maggie said. 'He didn't.'

Helen hesitated. 'You're stirring things up.'

Maggie looked at her. 'Things are already stirred.'

Helen sighed and said, 'Just be careful.' As she left, she called back over her shoulder,

'And don't let that coffee go cold.'

Maggie smiled with gratitude, watched her cross back to the café, then turned to the desk. Her hands remained steady, but her thoughts had realigned, connecting pieces that now seemed to fit. This was like solving a jigsaw puzzle. She didn't wait for the library to empty before closing the office door again. She retrieved the folder, added a note about Ridley's visit, and tucked it into her bag.

By the time she locked the library and stepped outside, she had made her decision. Instead of heading home, she headed toward the river along a longer route that bypassed the old access track. The uneven ground and poorly maintained path, which differed from the council maps, made her move carefully, remaining alert for any movement or sounds.

The river was calmer here, narrower, with its surface disturbed by branches and debris caught along the bank. Maggie stopped where the path dipped, examining the ground. Noticing tyre marks, fresh tyre marks.

Maggie crouched down, observing where the tracks approached the water before turning back toward the trees. It was clear someone had recently driven through, either with permission or with enough confidence to do so. She stood up, her heart racing—not from fear, but from certainty. This was no coincidence. It wasn't erosion. It was deliberate control.

A sound behind her made her turn sharply.

Maureen stood a short distance back, arms folded, eyes sharp. 'I thought you might come this way.'

Maggie exhaled. 'You followed me.'

'I worried you'd do something foolish alone,' Maureen said. Her gaze dropped to the ground. 'They've been here, haven't they?'

'Yes, it appears so'

Maureen shook her head slowly. 'I've lived here long enough to know when the council's tidying up more than paperwork.'

They stood together for a moment, the weight of it settling between them.

'I'm not asking you to help,' Maggie said.

Maureen smiled faintly. 'Good. Because I was going to offer anyway.'

Maggie nodded, accepting it without ceremony.

Maureen didn't stay once they left the riverbank. She accompanied Maggie to the main road, then paused, hands on her hips, inspecting the bushes between the track and the water as if she thought it might shift if she watched long enough.

'I won't say anything,' Maureen said. 'Not unless you ask me to.'

'I won't,' Maggie replied. 'Not yet.'

Maureen nodded once, satisfied, and

turned back toward town without another word.

Maggie continued home alone, her attention split between the path ahead and the quiet recalculations in her mind. Council vehicles near the river. A man sent to ask about Arthur's library use. Records being adjusted after Arthur's death. Tyre tracks close to the bank, suggesting intent rather than accident. None of it proved anything on its own. Together, though, the pieces were beginning to resist the story everyone wanted to believe.

Martin was in the shed when she arrived home, the radio murmuring low behind the scrape of wood on wood. He looked up as she crossed the yard, reading her face before she spoke.

'They've been down near the access track,' Maggie said, skipping preamble.

Martin wiped his hands on a rag. 'Council?'

'Yes.'

He frowned. 'After the police said everything was done?'

'Yes.'

He leaned back against the workbench. 'That's not usual.'

'No,' Maggie agreed. 'Is asking me about Arthur's computer use?'

Martin was quiet for a moment. 'What are you thinking?'

'That someone's trying to make sure nothing surfaces that shouldn't.' Maggie set her bag down and took out the folder. She didn't open it yet. 'And that they're not as confident as they're pretending to be.'

Martin exhaled slowly. 'You're past the point of curiosity now.'

'Yes,' Maggie said. 'I know.'

***

They had dinner quietly, with their usual

evening routines. After dinner, while Martin washed the dishes, Maggie sat at the table and spread the folder's contents, aligning the pages so they formed a coherent whole. It really did resemble a jigsaw puzzle in its early stages, with the image still obscured but the edges beginning to emerge.

She didn't rush. She never rushed puzzles. There was always a temptation to force pieces that almost fit, but she'd learned long ago that patience was faster in the end.

The adjusted library record sat beside Arthur's notes. The dates overlapped too neatly to ignore. Someone had reacted, not discovered. That distinction mattered.

Later, Maggie lay awake in bed, her thoughts no longer circling but following lines, exploring different directions. The Council didn't panic without cause, nor did they close areas without cause. Not unless there was something hidden they didn't want found.

The next day, Maggie returned to work with a sense of purpose. She first checked the roster, then the staff log, and finally the back-office calendar. She reviewed records that she seldom used, which most people overlooked because they were dull and procedural, such as access permissions, temporary logins, and audit trails.

Someone had accessed Arthur's borrowing record again. Not to change it this time. To view it. The access wasn't traced to a staff login. It came through an external portal, authorised but rarely used. Maggie stared at the screen, then printed the page without hesitation. She added it to the folder, her movements precise.

Another staff member appeared at the office door. 'You've got company.'

Maggie stepped out to find Senior

Constable Harris waiting near the counter. He looked tired, less settled than he had before.

'Maggie,' he said. 'Do you have a moment?'

'I do,' she replied. 'Here.'

They spoke at the side desk, where it was more private. Harris cleared his throat.

'I've had a call from the council,' he said. 'They're concerned about speculation.'

Maggie raised an eyebrow. 'Speculation about what?'

'Arthur's death,' Harris said. 'They want it settled.'

'And you?' Maggie asked.

Harris hesitated. 'I want it accurate.'

'So you want to find the truth now?'

'I was wrong before. There's more to Arthur's death, isn't there?'

Maggie slid the printed page across to him. 'Then you should look at this.'

He scanned it, his jaw tightening. 'This access—'

'Wasn't me,' Maggie said. 'And it wasn't staff.'

Harris looked up. 'Why would anyone be checking a dead man's library record?'

'That's what I'd like to know,' Maggie replied.

Harris folded the paper carefully. 'I need to make a call.'

'Of course,' Maggie said.

He paused. 'Maggie. Be careful.'

'I am,' she said. 'I'm just not stopping.'

When he left, Maggie's resolve firmed. She'd stepped into a space where she couldn't pretend neutrality anymore. That line was behind her now.

Later, as she locked up for the day, she glanced once more towards the river, but the water gave nothing away.

She turned the key, slipped the folder into her bag, and walked on, already assembling the next piece in her mind. The picture was forming.

Chapter Fourteen

Maggie added another piece to the jigsaw on the kitchen table and paused with her fingers on the cardboard. It wasn't because the picture suddenly made sense, but because she realised she'd been pushing the edges without realising it. The piece fit fairly well, but it wasn't correct. She took it out, placed it aside, and left the gap empty.

Martin came in with two mugs of tea and raised an eyebrow at the unfinished corner. 'That's unlike you.'

'What, making mistakes?' Maggie grinned

Martin set a mug beside her and leaned a hip against the bench. 'Are we talking about the puzzle or everything else?'

Maggie didn't answer directly. She slid the box lid back on and pushed the whole thing further up the table, making room for the day ahead. 'We should go.'

'People will be there already,' Martin said.

'That's fine,' Maggie replied. 'It's a working bee, not a parade.'

The working bee had been organised quickly, and that was the first thing that bothered Maggie. Wattle River could be slow to act on most things, especially anything that required coordination, but it could move with startling speed when there was an image to protect. Clean tracks, a tidy town, community spirit, and a positive story in the local paper about people coming together after a sorrowful week. She understood the impulse. She even respected it, in a way. What she didn't trust was how convenient it was.

***

At the trailhead, a small group had already assembled. There were gloves, garbage bags, grabbers, and a folding table with a cheerful handwritten sign saying **THANK YOU VOLUNTEERS** in block letters. Two council-branded buckets stood beneath it, spotless and seemingly reserved for the photo rather than actual use.

Evelyn Crowe stood by the table, wearing a wide-brimmed hat and holding a clipboard, greeting arrivals. She appeared perfectly suited for her position: poised, approachable, and effortlessly calm. Maggie observed how instinctively the group turned toward her, waiting for her nod before proceeding, as if she was the vital focus of the morning.

Evelyn turned and spotted Maggie. Her smile came easily, warm and unforced. 'Maggie. Martin. I'm so glad you've come.'

'We're here to pick up rubbish,' Martin

said, polite but firm, as if he'd decided in advance not to be folded into anything else.

Evelyn laughed softly. 'And that's exactly what we'll do. Nothing complicated.' Her gaze settled on Maggie. 'It's good for the town to do something together.'

Maggie nodded, giving nothing away. 'How many sections are you covering?'

Evelyn tapped the clipboard. 'We'll start with the main walking tracks. The loop and the lookout. The idea is to make it safe and pleasant for families again. People have been avoiding the area since… well.'

Since Arthur, Maggie thought, but Evelyn didn't mention his name. She rarely named him, especially in public. She maintained a smooth facade by keeping things vague.

Evelyn continued, still smiling. 'And council has arranged a skip at the end of the track. We'll keep it simple.'

A man whispered something to Evelyn. Maggie heard only a few words: Access, Council, and down near the bend.

Evelyn's expression didn't change, but the hand holding the clipboard tightened briefly before relaxing. She nodded once and replied in a tone that sounded reassuring from a distance. 'Not today. We're focusing on the public sections.'

The man moved away.

Maggie glanced at Martin. He had seen it too. Though he said nothing, his gaze held hers for a bit longer than usual, silently asking a question.

Evelyn turned back quickly. 'All right, everyone. Gloves on. If you're new to this, pair up. If you see anything sharp, don't pick it up with your hands. Use the grabber stick to bring it to the council bins or tell me.'

People began to sort themselves into pairs.

Maureen arrived with a roll of heavy-duty bags and looking determined. Helen came too, which surprised Maggie, given that the café was usually busy, but Helen looked like she'd made a point of being here.

June Wallace stood off to one side with her arms crossed, her eyes shifting between Evelyn and the track ahead. She offered Maggie a subtle nod.

Maggie and Martin were assigned a stretch along the main track, the busiest one for casual walks. It suited Maggie well. The more public the area, the less likely she was to get involved in anything that would make her seem as though she had other reasons for being there besides picking up litter.

They worked consistently, collecting bottle caps, wrappers, sun-faded thongs, and plastic scraps caught in the grass. The task was simple enough that people talked, and Maggie soon realised this working bee was a typical activity in small towns. It allowed people to talk about their burdens without feeling the need to admit they needed to.

'Poor Arthur,' someone said up ahead, voice softened.

'Yes,' someone else replied. 'But at least it would have been quick. I would have hated him to suffer.'

A woman Maggie didn't know well but had seen around town joined them for a while, quickly and efficiently picking up rubbish. 'I still can't believe he was down there,' she said, avoiding eye contact, as if speaking into the air made it safer. 'He wasn't the sort to wander.'

Maggie kept her focus on the edge of the track. 'People do things out of character when they're worried.'

The woman paused, then resumed, faster. 'True. I suppose. Still.'

Martin moved a little closer to Maggie, a quiet, protective motion that was unnoticeable but changed the shape of their small group.

Further ahead, Len was instructing two others about council maintenance and bank stability with his brisk depot-worker tone. Maggie didn't approach him but listened as she passed by.

'Funny thing,' Len was saying. 'They never worry about "erosion" until it suits them.'

One of the men laughed nervously. 'You always think it's a conspiracy.'

Len didn't smile. 'No. I think it's too much paperwork.'

Maggie kept walking.

At the lookout, Evelyn stood near the signboard, welcoming visitors, guiding them to various paths, which made her appear organised. She was skilled at it. This didn't indicate guilt; instead, it demonstrated competence, and Maggie understood that this skill could be risky if misused.

Helen appeared beside Maggie, a bag half-full of rubbish in hand, her face suggesting she was keeping her temper on a short leash. 'You noticed the way she redirected that bloke, didn't you?'

Maggie didn't pretend. 'Yes, I did.'

Helen lowered her voice. 'I'm not saying anything. I'm just saying it's interesting.'

'It is,' Maggie agreed.

Helen's eyes narrowed. 'And council doesn't do interesting without a reason.'

Before Maggie could respond, a call went up from further along the track.

'Evelyn! We've got a problem.'

Heads turned. Bodies shifted. The sound carried that specific kind of small-town urgency, the kind that fed itself because it was witnessed.

Evelyn moved quickly, not running, but decisive. 'What is it?'

A teenage boy stood near a cluster of shrubs, holding a torn garbage bag away from his body as if it might bite. 'There's broken glass everywhere. Someone's dumped a whole box of bottles down the side.'

Evelyn stepped close enough to assess but not close enough to touch. 'All right,' she said, voice calm. 'Nobody goes down the slope. We'll mark it off and deal with it properly. Where's the tape?'

Tape, Maggie observed—Evelyn was practical and organised, someone who anticipated problems and had solutions prepared.

A council worker produced a roll. Evelyn directed him to cordon the area. 'We're not here to hurt ourselves,' she said with a brisk smile. 'We're here to make things better.'

People murmured approval and moved on.

Maggie kept collecting rubbish, but the scene stayed in her mind. Broken bottles thrown down a slope weren't the same as what she was thinking about, but they served as a distraction. They created a clear, solvable issue for the group to focus on, something everyone could agree was wrong without having to bring up deeper issues.

As they moved further along, the track narrowed, trees pressing closer. The sound of the town faded behind leaves and dirt. Maggie didn't like how quickly the group stretched out here. Volunteers drifted into small clusters, then broke apart again when the path split, people choosing the most convenient direction rather than the assigned one.

Evelyn had tried to keep it orderly, but order was never the true nature of a working bee. The truth of it was movement and people doing what they thought made sense in the moment.

Maureen caught up with Maggie, her bag already nearly full. 'This is bigger than it needed to be,' she muttered.

'Because it's not just about rubbish,' Maggie replied.

Maureen's eyes flicked toward Evelyn in the distance. 'She's making it about community.'

'And the council,' Maggie said.

Maureen's mouth tightened. 'Same thing, if you ask some people.'

They arrived at a fork where one route led to the lookout loop, while the other descended toward a lower trail that stayed closer to the river before merging again. A small sign indicated both directions. The lower trail was labelled as uneven, with a warning to be cautious.

A man Maggie recognised from town but didn't know personally stood there, hands on hips, looking down the lower path as if deciding something. He wore work boots, carried a grabber tool like a prop, and had the restless energy of someone who didn't enjoy being told where to go.

Evelyn's voice carried from further up. 'Stay on the main track, please. We're not going down on the lower section today.'

The man glanced back, nodded as if he'd heard, then waited until Evelyn's attention shifted and stepped down the lower path anyway.

Maggie watched him go, her stomach tightening. Martin noticed her gaze. 'Should we say something?'

Maggie shook her head. 'People only hear what they want.'

Maureen huffed. 'That one always thinks

rules are for someone else.'

Maggie took a breath, then turned deliberately towards the main track. She did not follow. She would not be the one chasing after others, not today. If she did, she'd be cast in the story as the one who couldn't let things go, and she didn't need the town handing her a label.

They continued, picking up rubbish, occasionally chatting to other volunteers. June drifted past, eyes sharp, and murmured, 'He shouldn't be down there,' before moving on again.

Maggie maintained her steady pace, not glancing back. Instead, she focused on listening, as she always did, and committing what she heard to memory.

For a while, all she heard was the scrape of grabbers, the rustle of leaves, the occasional laugh as someone found something odd and harmless. The community doing its best to be normal.

Then, from somewhere below and ahead, a voice rose, loud enough to draw attention from those in the vicinity.

'Oi! Evelyn!'

The call was sharper than before, edged with something more than mere inconvenience. People froze, then moved instinctively towards the sound.

Maggie's heart kicked once, hard.

Martin's hand found her elbow, steadying without restraining. 'That's him,' he said quietly.

Maggie nodded, already moving, not running but moving faster in the direction of the voices as the crowd began to shift. Whatever had happened down on the lower track, it had just become everyone's business.

The call caused the volunteers to move downhill quickly. She maintained a steady pace, allowing others to rush ahead while she observed.

The man who had ignored Evelyn's instructions stood partway down the slope, one hand braced against a tree, his grabber discarded at his feet. His face had lost its earlier confidence, colour draining as he gestured toward the riverbank below.

'There,' he said, voice rough. 'On the rock.'

Evelyn arrived moments later, breath even, eyes already assessing. She instinctively lifted a hand, stopping people from moving closer. 'All right,' she said, calm and clear. 'Everyone stay where you are.'

Maggie stopped several paces back. She didn't need to be closer to see it.

The rock sat just above the waterline, broad and pale where it jutted out from the bank. Against that pale surface was a dark smear, irregular, not fresh enough to glisten but not old enough to have faded into the stone. It followed the natural curve of the rock, as though something had been pressed there, then dragged.

Someone swore softly behind Maggie.

'That's blood,' the man said. 'Has to be.'

Evelyn didn't contradict him immediately. She stepped carefully closer, stopping short of the edge. She crouched, hands on her knees, studying the stain without touching it.

'It could be animal,' she said finally. 'Kangaroo, perhaps. They get injured, move through here.'

'On a rock?' someone asked.

'They rest,' Evelyn replied. 'They bleed.'

Her tone was reasonable. It didn't invite argument so much as convey exhaustion. Maggie felt it ripple through the group. People wanted that explanation. They wanted something that fit neatly into the version of events they'd already accepted.

Maggie said nothing. She watched instead.

Evelyn stood and turned to the group. 'We're not equipped to deal with this properly. I'll contact the council. In the meantime, no one touches anything.'

'Call the police, not the council,' said the man who'd discovered it.

'Well, of course, if you think that's necessary,' Evelyn replied.

She pulled her phone from her pocket and stepped a little way back, speaking quietly. Maggie couldn't hear the words, but she saw the posture: upright, composed, in control.

Maureen leaned in close. 'That's not animal blood,' she murmured.

'You don't know that,' Maggie replied gently.

'I know enough,' Maureen said. 'And so

do you.'

Maggie didn't answer. She was looking at the rock again, at the way the stain sat not at the lowest point, but higher, where someone would brace themselves if they were unsteady. She noted the faint scuff marks nearby, half obscured by dirt and leaves, as though someone had tried to kick debris over them.

June appeared beside them, arms folded tight across her chest. 'Someone's been down here before today.' June's eyes flicked to Evelyn. 'She knows it too.'

A police car arrived quicker than Maggie expected, crunching to a stop on the track above. Senior Constable Harris climbed out, followed by a younger officer Maggie didn't recognise. Harris took in the scene in one long look, then nodded at Evelyn.

'Thanks for calling it in,' he said.

'Of course,' Evelyn replied. Only her

pallor betrayed any discomfort.

Harris crouched near the rock while the younger officer took photos, noting angles and measuring distances. Harris straightened after a moment, his expression neutral.

'We'll take this for testing,' he said, bagging the rock into an evidence bag. 'But it's likely animal blood. There's nothing else here to suggest—'

'Except that Arthur was found not far from this stretch,' June said, unable to stop herself.

Harris looked at her, then at Maggie. 'Arthur wasn't found here.'

'No,' Maggie said. 'But he was near the river.'

Harris's jaw tightened slightly. 'We don't want to make any assumptions at this stage.'

Maggie met his gaze. 'We don't want to exclude anything either.'

Evelyn stepped in smoothly. 'Let's not

alarm people unnecessarily. This was meant to be a positive morning.'

Harris nodded, grateful for the assist. 'We'll handle it.'

The crowd began to disperse under Evelyn's direction, being redirected back towards the main track and reassured with calm words.

Maggie stayed where she was until the area cleared, with the rock now guarded by tape and the steady presence of the officers.

Harris approached her then, voice low. 'You're thinking this means something more.'

'I think someone meant to throw it into the river,' Maggie replied. 'And didn't do a good enough job.

He sighed. 'That's an assumption.'

'It is,' Maggie agreed. 'So is animal blood.'

Harris studied her for a long moment.

'You're not wrong to ask questions. Just don't get ahead of the evidence.'

Maggie nodded. 'I won't. I'll wait for it to catch up.'

When they finally left, the working bee did not resume. People drifted away in small groups, the earlier sense of purpose replaced by unease. The tidy image the town had wanted had fractured, just enough to let doubt in.

Evelyn lingered near the trailhead, thanking volunteers, offering reassurances. When she reached Maggie, her smile was still in place, but it required more effort now.

'Unfortunate,' she said. 'But I'm sure it's nothing to do with Arthur.'

'Perhaps,' Maggie replied.

Evelyn's eyes held hers for a moment longer than necessary. 'You look tired.'

Maggie smiled faintly. 'It's been a week.'

'Yes,' Evelyn said. 'It has.'

On the walk back to the car, Martin spoke first. 'That wasn't nothing.'

'No,' Maggie said. 'And someone hoped it would be.'

Later, at home, Maggie stood at the kitchen table again. The jigsaw waited where she'd left it, the unfinished corner still open. She picked up the piece she'd set aside earlier, turned it once, and slid it into place. This time, it fit. The picture didn't change all at once. But it shifted enough that she could see where the next pieces might go.

Somewhere between the river and the records, between what was said and what was smoothed over, the truth was waiting.

And Maggie was no longer the only one who sensed it.

Chapter Fifteen

The call came before Maggie had finished her first cup of tea. Senior Constable Harris didn't waste words. 'I need to see you.'

'Where?' Maggie asked.

'Library,' he said. 'And I'd rather not make it look like an official visit.'

Maggie understood immediately. 'I'll meet you in the back room.'

When she arrived, Harris was already present, standing by the long table typically used by the Local History Group. He appeared tired in a way that went beyond simple exhaustion. His uniform was tidy, and his posture was steady, but there was a change in his expression since the working bee.

'This isn't off the record,' he said, before

she could speak. 'But it's not formal either.'

Maggie sat. 'That's a narrow line.'

'I'm getting used to them,' Harris replied.

He placed a thin folder on the table and opened it. Photographs slid into view: the rock by the river, the stain, the taped boundary, the surrounding ground.

'Preliminary tests came back,' he said. 'Not animal blood.'

Maggie's breath slowed, not caught. 'Human?'

'Yes.'

'That doesn't make it Arthur's,' Harris continued. 'Not on its own. But it changes the category.'

'From unlikely to inconvenient,' Maggie said.

'From closed to open,' Harris corrected.

She nodded. 'What else?'

Harris hesitated, then pushed another sheet

forward. 'The access track. Council maintenance logs don't match vehicle movement. There's been activity there that wasn't recorded.'

Maggie looked at him steadily. 'So someone's been there without paperwork.'

'Yes.'

'And the car?' she asked.

Harris exhaled slowly. 'Still missing.'

Silence sat between them, quiet yet clear.

'Arthur didn't fall,' Maggie said quietly.

Harris didn't contradict her.

'What made you change your mind?' she asked.

'I didn't,' Harris said. 'I changed my certainty.'

Maggie absorbed that. 'Those aren't the same thing.'

He leaned back slightly. 'Someone altered Arthur's library record. Council staff accessed his file after his death. A restricted track shows unlogged vehicle movement. Blood has been found on a rock near the river. That's not yet conclusive evidence of foul play, but it is …'

'It's a start,' Maggie finished for him.

Harris gave a faint smile. 'Exactly.'

He closed the folder. 'I need you to tell me everything Arthur was researching.'

Maggie didn't hesitate. 'Land records. Council minutes. Access boundaries. Historical lot divisions. Anything that touched the river corridor.'

'Did he tell you why?'

'No,' Maggie said. 'But he was close to something when his pages were removed.'

Harris's eyes sharpened. 'Removed.'

'Yes.'

'Deliberately.'

'Yes.'

Harris was quiet for a moment. 'Who had

access to his belongings?'

'Anyone in his house. Anyone who reached him before police.'

'Which could include—'

'Anyone with authority,' Maggie said.

Harris nodded once.

'Council?' he said.

Maggie and Harris never mentioned Evelyn's name. However, the unspoken distance between them changed subtly, as if a door that had been locked was now slightly ajar.

'What do you need from me?' Maggie asked.

Harris didn't answer immediately. He studied her for a moment, weighing something.

'I need you to keep doing what you're doing,' he said. 'But I need to know when you cross lines.'

Maggie's mouth curved faintly. 'I crossed those last week.'

'Yes,' Harris said. 'Which is why I'm here.'

He stood. 'And Maggie—'

'Yes?'

'Be careful who you trust.'

She met his gaze. 'Oh, don't worry about that part, people are starting to show their true colours.'

After he left, Maggie stayed at the table for a long moment, not thinking so much as calibrating. The investigation was no longer hers alone. That was a relief. It was also a risk.

When she returned to the main desk, she found Evelyn standing there, speaking with Helen. The timing was too neat to be a coincidence.

Evelyn turned, smile ready. 'Maggie. I was just asking whether there's been any update.'

Helen's eyes flicked between them.

'On what?' Maggie asked.

'The incident at the working bee,' Evelyn replied. 'People are asking questions. Naturally.'

'Are they?' Maggie said.

'Yes,' Evelyn said smoothly. 'Uncertainty unsettles people. It's kinder to give them clarity where we can.'

Maggie leaned lightly on the desk. 'And what clarity would you like them to have?'

Evelyn's smile softened. 'That it's being handled properly. That the town is safe. That there's no reason to imagine things that aren't supported by facts.'

Maggie nodded. 'That's always comforting.'

Evelyn held her ground. 'And responsible.'

'Sometimes,' Maggie said.

Evelyn studied her more closely now. 'You look tired.'

Maggie returned her look evenly.

Helen excused herself, leaving them alone at the desk.

'I hope you're not feeling burdened by any of this,' Evelyn said. 'People often project their worries onto the most reliable people.'

Maggie heard the meaning beneath the apparent kindness.

'I'm not burdened,' Maggie said. 'I'm just observant.'

Evelyn's smile tightened a fraction. 'Those can look similar from the outside.'

'Only if you're nervous,' Maggie replied.

Evelyn held her gaze for a moment longer than necessary. Then she nodded, composed again. 'If you hear anything from the police, I'd appreciate knowing.'

Maggie said nothing.

Evelyn turned and left.

From the doorway, June Wallace watched

her go.

'Well,' June said quietly. 'That was interesting.'

Maggie didn't answer.

June stepped closer. 'She's nervous.'

'She's certainly attentive,' Maggie said.

'Same thing,' June replied.

Maggie looked at her. 'Not always.'

June studied her. 'You don't trust her.'

'I don't trust anyone who needs to manage a story,' Maggie said.

June's eyes sharpened. 'Including the police?'

Maggie paused. 'Let's just say I don't believe everything I'm told by authorities.'

June nodded. 'Good.

***

Later, as the library quietened, Maggie went back to the back office and reopened the folder. She included a new page, recording only what she could substantiate.

Blood confirmed.

Access track movement unlogged.

Car still missing.

Council involvement increasing.

Police investigating.

She didn't write down any names, nor make any assumptions. She just wrote down the clues that had revealed themselves.

At home that evening, she sat at the table and reached for the jigsaw again. The puzzle was taking shape now, the image clearer, the empty spaces fewer. She fitted two pieces together and paused, seeing not the picture, but the pattern of what was still missing.

Somewhere between the river and the records, between council authority and police procedure, there was a person who had something to hide.

Was it something worth killing for? The

next shift came quietly. Not with an announcement or a knock at the door, but with a change in how people spoke to Maggie when they thought they were being careful.

It started with Helen, who brought her a coffee she hadn't asked for and left it on the desk with a look that suggested she'd rehearsed what she wanted to say and then abandoned it halfway through.

'They were talking at the café,' Helen said, as if that explained everything.

'Who?' Maggie asked.

'People,' Helen replied. 'About the working bee. About the police being back around the river.'

Maggie nodded. 'That was always going to happen.'

Helen leaned on the counter. 'It's different this time. Before, it was all... poor Arthur, terrible business, let's move on. Now they're wondering who knew what, and when.'

'And what are you wondering?' Maggie asked.

Helen gave a small, humourless smile. 'I'm wondering why the council's suddenly very interested in things they haven't cared about for years.'

Maggie said nothing. She didn't need to. Helen straightened and went back to the café, leaving the coffee cooling beside the keyboard.

***

Not long after, Senior Constable Harris returned, this time without calling ahead. He didn't come into the library proper. He waited just outside, near the noticeboard, visible but not intrusive. Maggie finished with a patron and stepped out to meet him.

'I've spoken to my sergeant,' Harris said. 'We're treating this as a suspicious death pending further enquiries.'

'That's a shift,' Maggie replied.

'It is,' he said. 'Quietly.'

She understood the qualifier. 'And the council?'

Harris exhaled. 'Less cooperative than they were yesterday.'

Maggie raised an eyebrow. 'That's quick.'

'People get defensive when routines change,' Harris said. 'Or when questions get closer to home.'

He hesitated, then added, 'I also need to ask you something.'

'Go ahead.'

'Did Arthur ever mention Evelyn Crowe to you?'

Maggie kept her face neutral. 'Only in the context of council decisions. He didn't single her out.'

Harris nodded. 'And you?'

'I haven't either,' Maggie said.

'That wasn't the question,' Harris replied.

Maggie met his gaze. 'I just notice patterns and people's demeanours.'

He shifted his weight from one foot to the other. 'I don't want you pushing this on your own.'

'I won't,' Maggie said. 'But as I said before, I won't step back either.'

Harris looked as though he wanted to argue, then didn't. 'If you see something, hear something—'

'I'll tell you,' Maggie said. 'As long as you tell me when things stop adding up on your end.'

He gave a faint smile. 'Deal.'

When he left, Maggie stood for a moment watching the space he'd occupied, aware of how visible even a quiet police presence made everything feel. The town would read it however it wanted, and by the time she closed the library for the day, the air felt charged in a way she hadn't felt before. Not tense exactly. Alert.

At home, she set her bag down and went straight to the table where the jigsaw waited. She didn't sit immediately. She studied it standing, the image now mostly formed, only a small cluster of pieces missing near the centre. She picked up one piece, turned it once, then set it down again without placing it. The picture was almost complete, but something was still off. Not missing but misaligned.

Martin watched her from the doorway. 'You're thinking.'

'Yes,' Maggie said. 'And I don't like where it's heading at the moment.'

He crossed the room and rested a hand on the back of her chair. 'You don't have to solve it tonight.'

'I know,' she said. 'But I need to know

where not to look.'

She moved the piece slightly, then tried another. This one slid into place without resistance.

There it was. She exhaled, slow and steady.

'What?' Martin asked.

'Arthur wasn't just looking at land,' Maggie said. 'He was looking at timing.'

Martin frowned. 'Timing of what?'

'Decisions. Approvals. Access. Who signed off on what, and when.' She tapped the table lightly. 'If someone wanted to move something like a car, evidence, anything, then they'd need more than opportunity. They'd need permission, or at least the appearance of it.'

Martin was quiet for a moment. 'Council.'

'Yes,' Maggie said. 'But not all of council. One person can move faster than a committee.'

Later that night, Maggie wrote again in her notebook. Not conclusions. Just recording what she knew so far and the questions she hadn't yet worked out answers for.

Who had the freedom to act without question?

Who had the most to lose if Arthur discovered something hidden?

What had Arthur already discovered?

She closed the notebook without answering them.

The town would wake tomorrow, still believing it was the same place it had been a week ago. Familiar. Predictable. Safe. But Maggie knew better now. The investigation was no longer about whether Arthur's death had been an accident. That question had already been answered. The question now was who had been confident enough to make it look like one?

Chapter Sixteen

Harris had phoned and asked that Maggie meet him urgently up the river. She headed there without hesitation. *What had he found?*

Maggie saw the ute before she saw him, parked at an awkward angle near the river access track where the gravel thinned into clay and the trees pressed in. It wasn't a marked spot, just a place locals used when they wanted a quiet place to throw in a line or sit and contemplate life. Harris stood with his hands on his hips, staring down the slope as if the river might confess if he waited long enough.

She pulled in behind him and got out. The air smelled damp and sharp, the kind of smell that clung to your clothes. Maggie followed his gaze toward the bend upstream, where the current slowed and debris gathered after a rise. From here, the river looked ordinary. That was the trouble with it. Ordinary things could hide a lot.

'You've got something,' she said.

Harris nodded without looking at her. 'Anonymous tip-off. Just saw metal caught in a snag once the water dropped back.

'Metal?'

'Wheel rim,' Harris said. 'Or part of one.'

Her stomach tightened. 'Upstream?'

'Upstream,' he confirmed. 'Near the bend before the old causeway.'

They moved together down the track, Harris leading, Maggie careful where she placed her feet. The ground was soft in patches, churned where tyres had cut through earlier in the week. She noticed the marks without commenting, filed them away with the other things she hadn't said yet.

The river came into view in fragments through the trees. Paperbarks leaned over the bank, their roots exposed in places where the water had pulled at them. Branches and leaves had collected at the bend, caught where the current slowed and curled back on itself. Harris slowed, raised a hand.

'Stay there.'

Maggie stood beside him and looked.

Initially, it appeared as a simple shape among the branches—dark, angular, and off. Then, the angle changed, revealing the curved edge and the unmistakable line of a wheel rim caught against a fallen limb, partially submerged and partially visible. The river flowed past it, calm and indifferent.

Harris let out a breath he'd probably been holding since the call came in. 'Right,' he said.

'That's it.'

Maggie didn't answer. She didn't need to. The answer they had been waiting for had finally arrived.

Harris stepped back and pulled out his phone. 'I'm calling this in properly,' he said. 'Recovery, forensics, the works. I want this logged from the moment it's touched.'

Maggie nodded and remained in her spot. Her eyes shifted to the bank, focusing on the area above the waterline where the vegetation was sparse. She noticed a patch of grass that was flattened in an unusual way—pressed down and slow to bounce back. A few metres ahead, she saw a strip of dark fabric caught on a branch, torn at one end. It was small and easy to overlook unless you were attentive to signs of effort rather than just accidents.

Harris finished his call, pocketed his

phone, and his posture shifted from casual to focused. He no longer seemed to be waiting, but rather intent on what was happening.

'Don't touch anything,' he said, though she hadn't moved. 'I'll get tape up once backup arrives.'

'Of course,' Maggie said.

He glanced at her, then back to the river. 'If that's his car…'

'It matches what he drove,' Maggie said carefully.

Harris nodded. 'We'll confirm. But yes.'

They paused in silence as the water filled the gap between them. Maggie's thoughts organised themselves smoothly, fitting the pieces without strain. The rock had already been bagged and removed. Human blood was confirmed, but the match was still unresolved. The autopsy was delayed somewhere in a queue. And now, this.

'Someone put it here,' she said at last.

Harris didn't contradict her. 'It didn't float itself upstream.'

'No,' Maggie agreed. 'And it didn't come to rest like this by chance.'

Harris followed her gaze to the flattened grass, the torn fabric. He crouched, careful not to step too close, and studied the marks. 'Looks like weight,' he said. 'Something heavy being shifted.'

'Or guided,' Maggie said.

He straightened and looked at her. 'You thinking one person?'

'I'm thinking someone helped,' she replied. 'Even if they didn't know what they were helping with.'

Harris's jaw tightened. 'That fits.'

A car door slammed somewhere behind them. Maggie turned as a council vehicle pulled up at the top of the track, dust puffing around its tyres. Two figures climbed out. One she recognised immediately.

Evelyn paused when she saw the river, her expression smoothing into concern. She walked toward them, shoes unsuited to the ground, careful where she stepped.

'Constable,' she said, voice warm. 'I heard there was some sort of disturbance.'

Harris didn't return the warmth. 'This is a police matter, Evelyn. I need you to stay back from the bank.' He didn't bother to correct her in regard to him being a Senior Constable.

Her gaze flicked past him, just for a moment, toward the bend. The snag. The shape in the water. It was quick. Almost nothing. Maggie saw it anyway. 'Oh,' Evelyn said. 'Of course. I only wanted to see if there was anything the council could assist with.'

'Not at this stage,' Harris replied.

She nodded, hands clasped in front of her,

composure intact. 'We wouldn't want rumours starting.'

Harris met her eyes. 'That's not our concern.'

Something shifted then, subtle but real. Evelyn took a step back. Maggie felt it like a change in pressure.

Another police vehicle arrived, then another. Harris moved into action, setting a boundary, directing people where to stand and where not to. The riverbank became a crime scene, the ordinary transformed by attention and tape.

Maggie stayed close but out of the way. She watched as Harris spoke quietly to a council staffer who had arrived too quickly to be a coincidence. The man talked with his hands, too eager, offering information no one had asked for.

'I unlocked the gate earlier,' he said, voice

carrying despite himself. 'For maintenance. Just routine. Didn't think—'

Harris's head snapped up. 'Which gate?'

The man faltered. Maggie felt the click in her chest, sharp and certain.

Harris held up a hand. 'Stop. We'll talk about that properly in a minute.'

The man swallowed and nodded, colour draining from his face.

Maggie looked back to the river. The car sat where the current allowed it, patient as the water moved around it.

Senior Constable Harris wasted no time. As soon as the tape went up and the first marked vehicle arrived, he shifted into command without announcement or fuss. Radios crackled. Instructions were given in short, precise bursts.

Maggie stayed where he'd indicated, just outside the taped line, close enough to see but not close enough to interfere. She recognised the rhythm of this part of the job, the way Harris kept things moving before curiosity could harden into speculation. Already, people were gathering at the top of the track, drawn by the sight of vehicles and uniforms. Word would spread regardless. Harris was simply buying time.

Two uniformed officers approached the waterline carefully, stopping where Harris directed. One crouched to examine the snag holding the car in place while the other documented from a distance. Photos were taken. Maggie watched them work, noting how the branches had been forced aside rather than broken, bent under pressure and left that way. The car hadn't drifted in and lodged itself. It had been guided, nudged until the current could be trusted to finish the job.

A forensic officer arrived next, pulling on

gloves as she walked. Harris briefed her quickly, his voice low but firm. Maggie caught fragments as they spoke.

'Human blood confirmed on the rock… match pending… autopsy delayed… vehicle potentially linked.' The words landed with weight now that there was something solid to attach them to.

Evelyn remained at the edge of the gathering, speaking quietly to another council member. Her posture was composed, but her hands were clenched together tightly enough that her knuckles had gone pale. Maggie watched her listen, nod, then glance back toward the river as if checking whether the car was still there.

The council staffer Harris had cut off earlier hovered nearby, clearly unsure whether to leave or stay. Harris turned to him again, voice clipped. 'You said you unlocked a gate.'

'Yes,' the man said quickly. 'For maintenance. There was debris reported near the upper track after the water rose. I didn't think—'

'Which gate?' Harris repeated.

'The service access. The one council uses for bank inspections.'

Harris nodded once. 'And you logged that?'

The man hesitated. 'I… I was going to. I just hadn't—'

Harris didn't raise his voice. He didn't need to. 'We'll go through that properly. For now, you're not to leave. Understood?'

The man nodded, sweat beading at his temples.

Maggie sensed the pieces shift once more. Access. Timing. Assistance that didn't seem like help at the time. People performing small tasks simply because they were asked to, finding it easier than questioning the reasons behind it.

Harris stepped closer to Maggie, lowering his voice. 'We're treating this as a crime scene now.'

She met his gaze. 'Quietly?'

'For as long as we can,' he said. 'Once that car comes out, it won't stay quiet.'

They both looked back toward the water, where recovery equipment was being carried down the track. Ropes were laid out with care. A winch cable was fed slowly, guided by gloved hands.

Maggie watched the process unfold as the cable tightened, and the water around the snag shifted. Branches groaned softly as the pressure changed. A slick of dark oil bloomed briefly on the surface before thinning and drifting away.

'There,' one of the officers said. 'Rear quarter panel.'

The car moved, just enough to confirm its shape. Maggie's breath caught despite herself. She had expected this moment, but expectation didn't blunt its impact.

Harris gave a short nod. 'That's enough for now. We'll stabilise it before full recovery.'

He turned as another tilt tray truck pulled in, this one unmarked. A man stepped out, older than Harris, his manner brisk. 'Senior Constable,' the man said. 'I'm here for the vehicle recovery.'

Harris briefed him quickly, keeping his gestures to a minimum. Maggie took the opportunity to step a little closer to the bank, stopping where the tape allowed. From this angle, she could see more clearly the scrape marks in the mud where weight had shifted, and the faint lines that suggested something heavy had been eased down the slope rather than dropped.

She straightened as Harris joined her again. 'This wasn't panic,' she said quietly. 'At least, not all of it.'

Harris exhaled. 'No. Someone thought this through just enough to think it would work.'

'And trusted the river to finish it.'

He glanced at her. 'You keep saying that like it matters.'

'It does,' Maggie replied. 'People here believe the river cleans things. Carries them away. Makes them someone else's problem.'

Harris considered that, then nodded. 'And that belief did half the work for them.'

A sudden murmur rippled through the onlookers as the car shifted again, more of it emerging from the water now. Someone swore under their breath. Another covered their mouth.

Evelyn turned away.

Maggie noticed the timing. She always

noticed timing.

Harris noticed it too. 'I need to speak to her,' he said.

'Not yet,' Maggie replied. 'Let the car come up first. Let the facts do the talking.'

He looked at her for a long moment, then gave a slight nod. 'You're right.'

The winch tightened once more. Slowly, steadily, the car began to lift, water streaming from its underside, debris falling away as it emerged. The crowd fell silent, the only sound the hum of machinery and the rush of the river reclaiming its shape.

There would be no neat explanation now. No tidy ending anyone could repeat to make themselves feel better.

Maggie watched the car rise and felt the final piece settle into place.

The river had not erased what happened here. It had only held it, waiting for someone to look properly.

***

The recovery took longer than Maggie expected because Harris refused to rush it. Every movement was deliberate. Every adjustment was checked, then checked again. The car was stabilised first, secured against the current before it was lifted any further, the river still pushing at it as if reluctant to give it up.

Maggie stood back, arms folded loosely, watching the work unfold. The noise of the winch, the low voices, the scrape of metal against stone—all of it grounded her. This was no longer theory. It was evidence.

As the car rose higher, more of it emerged from the water. Mud streamed from the undercarriage. Leaves and river weed clung to the doors. One rear light hung shattered, its edges dulled by water rather than impact. Maggie's eyes moved over it carefully, noting what wasn't there as much as what was. No sign of a collision. No crumpling. No explanation that pointed to an accident rather than intention.

Harris moved between the recovery team and the edge of the scene, maintaining the boundary. He spoke briefly to a uniformed officer, then turned back toward Maggie.

'It's consistent,' he said quietly. 'No front-end damage. No skid marks leading down. If it went in from here, it was guided.'

Maggie nodded. 'And whoever did it didn't want it to travel far.'

'Or be found quickly,' Harris said.

A second call came in, this one routed directly to Harris. He listened, his expression unreadable, then ended the call and slipped the phone back into his pocket.

'That was forensics,' he said. 'They've expedited the blood analysis. Still waiting on confirmation, but the preliminary comparison is strong.'

'Arthur,' Maggie said.

'Yes,' Harris replied. 'They're not saying it officially yet. But it's heading that way.'

The words settled between them. Maggie felt the familiar tightening in her chest, the one that came when uncertainty narrowed into something sharper. She glanced back at the car as it was eased onto the tilt tray, tyres slick with river mud.

Evelyn had moved again. She stood with another council member near the vehicles, speaking in low tones. Maggie watched as she gestured toward the riverbank, then toward the track, as if outlining a version of events that would make sense.

Harris followed Maggie's gaze. 'She's trying to manage it.'

'She likes to be in control.'

Harris studied her face. 'You're certain?'

Maggie knew what he was implying. 'As certain as I can be without a confession.'

The recovery team paused, repositioning the straps. One of them swore softly as the winch cable caught, then freed it with a tug. The car shifted, settling more fully onto the bank. Water pooled beneath it, dark and slow-moving.

A uniformed officer approached Harris, notebook in hand. 'Senior Constable, we've got an issue with access logs.'

Harris turned. 'Go on.'

'The service gate was unlocked that night, but the electronic record shows a later timestamp than it should. Someone adjusted it.'

Maggie felt the click again, clean and unmistakable. 'After Arthur was already dead.'

The officer hesitated, then nodded. 'Yes.'

Harris's jaw set. 'Who has clearance to make that adjustment?'

'Council administration,' the officer

replied. 'And IT support.'

Harris glanced back toward Evelyn. This time, he didn't look away.

'Right,' he said. 'We'll follow up.'

The car was now fully out of the water and loaded onto the tow truck. Its registration plate was visible beneath the grime. Harris read it aloud, then nodded once.

'That's Arthur's.'

A murmur rippled through the small cluster of officers and staff. Phones were raised and quickly lowered again under Harris's sharp look. The scene tightened, the casual edges gone.

Maggie stepped closer, stopping at the tape. She leaned slightly to look through the driver's-side window. The interior was dark and waterlogged, with a smell of oil and river. The seats were intact. The steering column was undamaged. There was nothing here to suggest a man had lost control. Besides, it was a fair way upstream from where Arthur had been found. He wouldn't have walked that far along a slippery riverbank after an accident.

'Keys,' she said quietly.

Harris followed her line of sight. The ignition was empty.

'Which means,' he said.

'He didn't drive it in,' Maggie finished. 'And whoever moved it kept them.'

Harris nodded. 'Or disposed of them separately.'

Another officer approached. 'I just had a call about the rock. Forensics are confident it's a single impact point,' the officer continued. 'The pattern's consistent with a blow from behind.' Harris's expression didn't change, but Maggie felt the shift anyway. The last thread holding the official story together had frayed.

'Thank you,' Harris said.

The officer moved away. Harris turned back to Maggie. 'Once the autopsy confirms there was no cardiac event, we're done pretending this was anything but murder.'

Maggie nodded. 'And the motive?'

Harris's gaze flicked again toward Evelyn, who had gone very still. 'That's where your records come in.'

Maggie allowed herself a brief, steadying breath. 'Right.'

Harris straightened, voice lifting slightly as he addressed the team. 'All right. We're escalating this. Scene stays closed. Vehicle to be transported for full examination. I want timelines reconstructed and access logs locked down. No one alters anything from this point on.'

He turned back to Maggie once more. 'I'll need you.'

She met his eyes. 'I'm not going anywhere

now. I want to see the truth come out and justice for Arthur.'

As the car was prepared for transport, Maggie stepped back and let the scene move without her. The river flowed on, reshaping itself around the absence it had been forced to give up. Whatever people had believed about it—about what it could hide or wash away- no longer mattered.

This wasn't the river's doing.

Chapter Seventeen

Maggie didn't go straight home. She drove past the turn-off without realising she'd missed it, her hands steady on the wheel while her thoughts raced ahead, laying out possibilities, checking them, discarding them. By the time she noticed, the road had narrowed, and the trees had closed in, the river somewhere off to her left, unseen but close enough for her to feel it through the ground.

She slowed, then pulled over, letting the engine idle while she sat there and breathed. Not because she was overwhelmed, but because she'd learned the value of stopping before rushing into the next thing. Arthur had done the same. He'd taken his time, worked quietly, and trusted that the truth would show itself if you gave it space.

And now the river had done just that.

She turned the car around and headed back towards town, taking the longer route this time, looping past the older houses and the edge of the industrial strip before feeding back towards the centre. It gave her time to think and distance herself from the image of the car rising out of the water, heavy, dripping, and undeniable.

By the time she parked outside her house, the light had shifted. Afternoon was slipping towards evening, the shadows longer now, less forgiving. She went inside, dropped her bag on the chair by the door, and stood still for a moment, listening to the quiet.

She casually made tea, letting the kettle boil as she leaned against the bench, gazing out the window. The jigsaw puzzle remained where she left it earlier, with pieces arranged neatly and the image gradually becoming clearer. She didn't start working on it yet; that would happen later, when she needed something stable and tangible to ground her thoughts. For now, she wanted to track one last line of thinking while it was still vivid.

She brought her mug into the living room and sat down, pulling Arthur's notebook from her bag and placing it on the table. It wasn't the official files or the copies she prepared for Harris, but the one Arthur personally carried. The pages were worn, and edges were softened with use. This was not a man who hurried; he took his time to write down what mattered, and only then.

She turned the pages slowly, pausing where his handwriting shifted slightly, becoming tighter and more deliberate. That was when she noticed he was beginning to realise something was off. Dates. Lot numbers. Small notes in the margins that seemed insignificant alone but gained meaning when seen as a whole. Maggie gently ran a finger beneath one entry and then another, not so much reading as recalling what she already understood.

Arthur didn't set out to find corruption; he accidentally uncovered it while being cautious and assisting others.

Her phone buzzed on the table. She didn't jump. She picked it up, glanced at the screen, and felt a slight tightening in her chest.

Harris.

She answered. 'Maggie speaking.'

'We've secured the vehicle,' he said. 'Transported to the yard. Full forensic exam will start first thing tomorrow.'

'Good,' Maggie replied.

There was a pause, then, 'I didn't want to call you back down here unless I had to.'

'That's okay,' she said. 'What is it?'

'The council staffer we spoke to earlier, the one at the gate, he's nervous,' Harris said. 'Too nervous. He's asked for legal advice already.'

Maggie nodded, even though Harris couldn't see it. 'Because he's realised he didn't just unlock a gate.'

'Yes,' Harris said. 'He thinks he's going to be blamed for more than he understands.'

'He won't be, will he?' Maggie asked. 'He helped without knowing what he was helping with.'

'That's where this gets complicated,' Harris replied. 'And where it stops being just about Evelyn.'

Maggie leaned back in her chair, staring at the ceiling. 'You're thinking accomplices.'

'I'm thinking people who made certain choices because it was easier than asking questions.'

'Then you're thinking about half the town,' Maggie said.

Harris exhaled. 'That's what I was afraid of.'

They sat with that for a moment.

'I'm not done yet,' Maggie said finally. 'There's still something I want to check.'

'Records?' Harris asked.

'Not the ones everyone's been staring at,' she replied. 'The ones that didn't make sense at the time.'

There was a pause. 'Be careful,' Harris said, then stopped himself. 'No. That's not what I mean. Just… don't be too fearless. You're a very clever woman, Maggie, but you're not the police'

'I won't be. I'm always careful.' Maggie said.

They ended the call, and Maggie sat there a little longer, the mug cooling in her hands.

Harris was right. This was bigger than one person. Evelyn had pulled the final thread herself, but the fabric had been weakened long before that.

She stood, gathered Arthur's notebook, and placed it back in her bag. Then she moved to the table by the window and sat down in front of the jigsaw. She fitted a piece into place, then another, letting the rhythm settle her thoughts.

Arthur had trusted the process. So would she.

And the process was about to expose more than one uncomfortable truth.

***

Maggie worked on the jigsaw until the light faded enough that she had to switch on the lamp beside the table. She didn't rush it. The picture was nearly there now—a coastal scene, all pale sky and water and scrubby grass - but the missing pieces mattered more than the finished image. They were the clues that brought it all together. The big picture.

She paused, holding a piece between her fingers, turning it slightly to see where it might fit. That's when it fell into place.

It wasn't a sudden epiphany or a surprising insight; rather, it was a quiet alignment. Arthur hadn't just been checking land records. He'd been checking timing.

She set the piece down without placing it and reached for her bag again, this time pulling out her own notebook. Not Arthur's, but hers. The one she used to analyse patterns beyond official paperwork. She flipped to a page she had begun days earlier and added a line beneath the existing notes.

Gate unlocked—when?

Access logs altered—after death.

Vehicle placed—before discovery

River trusted—to erase evidence

She stared at the list, then added another line.

Who benefits from delay?

That was the question no one had asked out loud yet.

The council staffer had unlocked the gate because he'd been told to. The logs had been adjusted because someone with authority had requested it. The vehicle had been guided into the river because someone believed time and water would take care of the rest. The delay wasn't accidental. It was the point.

Maggie shut the notebook and leaned back, rubbing her neck. She felt tired, but not exhausted, more like the tiredness that comes from sustained focus rather than confusion. It signified that she was near her goal.

Her phone buzzed again, this time with a message from Harris rather than a call.

We've got Evelyn secured overnight. Solicitor present. She's not talking yet.

Maggie typed back slowly. **She will. But not tonight.**

By now, she was familiar with Evelyn's type. Control didn't fade when circumstances changed; it intensified. It sought leverage, looked for angles, and found scapegoats.

Maggie pushed the chair back and rose, heading to the window. Outside, the street was quiet, with a few lights shining in nearby houses—everyday scenes happening without any indication of the change beneath. Tomorrow, it would be discussed. But tonight, the town remained silent.

She returned to the table and picked up Arthur's notebook once more, this time flipping to the back. The final pages appeared less organised, filled with notes scribbled at odd angles, question marks, and names crossed out with lines.

One page, though, was different. It listed three council departments. Planning. Infrastructure. Records. Beside each, Arthur had written a single word. 'Access.'

Maggie traced the letters with her eyes. He hadn't been chasing a single decision. He'd been mapping movement. Who could touch what? Who could change things quietly without raising alarms, and who couldn't?

A shiver ran down her spine, a chill unrelated to fear but to clarity. Evelyn hadn't acted alone out of desire, but out of necessity in relation to Arthur. But the rest of it? That had required cooperation. Or at least compliance.

Maggie sat back down and placed the jigsaw piece carefully where it belonged. It slid into place with a soft click, the image sharpening just enough to reveal what the rest would look like when it was finished.

She gave a faint smile, then her expression grew serious. Tomorrow, she planned to visit the only place she hadn't been back to since the recovery—not the library or the council chambers, but the records storage annex.

It wasn't a place people thought about much. Tucked behind the main council building, it was low and functional, mainly used by staff who wanted to stay inconspicuous. Arthur had spent time there, and she was aware of that now. Maggie had learned that truth seldom resides where people assume it does.

She finished her tea, rinsed the mug, and left it to dry. Then she gathered Arthur's notebook, her own, and her bag, placing everything neatly by the door for the morning.

Before turning off the light, she glanced again at the nearly finished jigsaw puzzle. It wasn't complete yet.

***

The records annex smelled faintly of dust and disinfectant. Maggie signed in at the desk without comment, accepted the temporary access badge, and walked down the narrow corridor towards the storage room at the back. The staff member on duty barely looked up, which told her plenty. People who worked with records learned early how to disappear into routine. Arthur had known that.

Inside the storage room, the temperature dropped slightly. Rows of compact shelving filled the space, each unit labelled with a careful, institutional precision. Maggie stood still for a moment, letting her eyes adjust, then moved toward the section Arthur had flagged in his notes.

Infrastructure access logs.

Archive transfers.

Internal authorisations.

This wasn't where decisions were made.

This was where decisions were disguised. She opened one of the shelves and searched through the boxes until she found the correct year, then moved on to the next, and then the following one. Arthur had been meticulous. His handwriting resurfaced repeatedly in the margins of photocopied documents, with small pencil marks next to entries that most would overlook. Maggie pulled one folder free and laid it open on the table.

Gate access: logged.

Adjustment timestamp: altered.

Authorisation: internal override.

She turned the page slowly.

There it was again.

Not a name. A role.

Temporary systems administrator.

Maggie exhaled through her nose, contemplating the nature of roles—they shift, overlap. She compared Arthur's notes with the document, noticing he'd circled the same designation three times—calmly, purposefully, understanding its significance.

She took photos of the page, ensuring the box label was visible, then repeated the process across different months, revealing a pattern of recurring behaviour.

As she was returning the folder, she spotted an unfiled, thin slip of paper in the back pocket of the box—unauthorised, lacking letterhead or stamps. Just a note. She unfolded it carefully.

'Access approved as discussed. Delete trail once completed.'

There was no signature, but the handwriting was neat and confident, somewhat familiar to Maggie in a way she couldn't quite identify. She chose not to return it to its original place; instead, she tucked it into her notebook and replaced the folder exactly as she had found it. After signing out, she stepped back into the daylight, blinking against the sudden brightness.

Harris was waiting outside in his car. He didn't wave or call to her. Instead, he just opened the passenger door. Maggie got in without comment. They sat in silence for a brief moment before he finally spoke.

'You find what you were looking for?' he asked.

'I found what Arthur was looking for,' she replied as she handed him the notebook and then the folded note.

He read it once and then again. 'This isn't new,' he said cautiously, 'but it's not insignificant either.' 'No,' Maggie agreed. 'It's leverage.' He nodded. 'And it indicates a direction away from Evelyn.'

'It points around her,' Maggie corrected. 'She's the centre, but she wasn't the one manipulating every lever.' Harris leaned back slightly, looking straight ahead. 'We already suspected that.' 'Yes,' Maggie confirmed. 'But now you have proof.'

He looked at her then, properly. 'You're doing my job for me.'

She didn't bristle. 'No. I'm doing it for Arthur.'

Harris folded the note and put it in his jacket pocket. 'There's more,' he said. 'The clerk we talked to yesterday? They recalled another name, not one Evelyn mentioned directly. Someone who gave instructions as a matter of course.'

Maggie waited.

'Internal IT,' Harris continued. 'Temporary contract. Been renewed quietly for years.'

Maggie's mouth tightened. 'Someone who knows how to change timestamps without triggering alerts.'

'Yes.'

'And who would panic now that Evelyn's in custody,' Maggie added.

Harris nodded once. 'Which is why we're going to let them make a mistake.'

Maggie didn't smile, but something seemed to settle all the same. She looked out the window as they drove, observing the familiar streets passing by. The town appeared unchanged.

Arthur was killed because he refused to overlook what seemed wrong, trusting the records more than the stories surrounding them. Due to his stubbornness, the structure Evelyn depended on began to break down, gradually and from within.

Harris pulled over near the station.

'I'll need you again,' he said. 'Not officially.'

Maggie nodded, realising that her part in

this was not yet over, and there were still loose ends to tie up and people who needed to be brought to justice. For Arthur.

Chapter Eighteen

Maggie was in the car when Harris rang. He didn't preface it, didn't soften it, didn't let the words settle gently. He simply said it.

'There was no cardiac event.'

She pulled over without thinking, the tyres crunching on gravel as she eased to the side of the road. The river was out of sight here, hidden behind trees and scrub, but she could feel its presence all the same, like a pressure she'd grown used to carrying.

'So the head injury,' she said.

'Yes,' Senior Constable Harris replied. 'Blunt force trauma. The pathologist's clear. The injury would have rendered him unconscious almost immediately.'

Maggie closed her eyes for a moment. Not in shock. Not in grief. In acknowledgement. This was the piece they'd been waiting on, the one that made everything else fall into line.

'When?' she asked.

'Preliminary estimate puts the injury before the collapse,' Harris said. 'There was no evidence of a heart attack. The narrative doesn't hold.'

She exhaled slowly. 'So it's official.'

'Yes,' Harris said. 'Arthur Bell was murdered.'

He let the silence sit for a moment. Maggie knew him well enough now to hear the shift in his voice, not urgency but authority.

He continued, 'I'm escalating it, classifying it as homicide. Warrants are being expanded, and records preservation orders are going out today.'

Maggie opened her eyes and looked ahead,

the road empty and pale under the sun. 'Council records too.'

'Yes,' Harris said. 'All of them. Planning, land use, access logs, and IT archives. Anything tied to rezoning or classification changes in the past fifteen years.'

'Evelyn won't like that.'

Harris gave a short, humourless sound. 'No. She won't.'

They ended the call a few minutes later. Maggie stayed where she was, hands resting lightly on the steering wheel. Murder changed things. It removed the last excuse people were clinging to. There would be no gentle explanations now, no comfort in repetition.

She drove on, not back to the library, but toward the edge of town where the land rose slightly before flattening again. The block sat behind a locked gate, scrub pushing in from all sides, the fence newer than it should have been for a parcel officially designated as low-value, non-developable land. She parked and walked the perimeter slowly.

The fence posts were recent. The wire was taut. Maggie stopped and looked closer, noting where old markers had been removed and replaced, the ground disturbed beneath them. A boundary that had shifted just enough to matter, if you knew what you were looking for.

She crouched and brushed dirt away from one of the posts. Beneath it, faint but still legible, was the scar where the original marker had been driven decades earlier. This land had been redrawn, and not on paper alone.

Her phone buzzed again. This time it was a text from Harris.

Can you come to the council chambers? Now?

She locked the gate behind her and drove back toward town. The council building was already busy when she arrived, marked cars out front and people standing just a little too close together, talking in low voices that stopped when she passed.

Inside, Harris stood near the reception desk, speaking quietly to an officer. He turned when he saw Maggie and gestured for her to come over.

'We've got a problem,' he said.

'Which one?' Maggie asked, 'Or are they blending together now?'

He didn't smile. 'A clerk tried to access archived planning files this morning. Off-hours credentials. They panicked when the system flagged it.'

Maggie's pulse quickened. 'Did they get in?'

'No,' Harris said. 'But they tried to cover the attempt. Claimed it was routine maintenance.'

'And it wasn't.'

'It never is,' Harris said. 'What's interesting is who authorised their access.'

He handed Maggie a printout. Not a report. A simple log.

One name sat at the top.

Evelyn Crowe.

Maggie looked at it carefully, then handed it back. 'She's moving.'

'Yes,' Harris said. 'And she's slipping. The pressure is making her careless.'

As if summoned by the thought, Evelyn appeared at the far end of the corridor, heels clicking sharply against the tiles. She took in the sight of them—Maggie, Harris, the officers and adjusted her expression into something composed and pleasant.

'Senior Constable,' she said, emphasising the Senior. 'I heard there was some confusion this morning.'

Harris didn't step toward her. He didn't invite her closer either. 'There was an attempted access to restricted files.'

Evelyn's brow furrowed. 'That's unfortunate. I'll have it addressed.'

'You won't,' Harris replied evenly. 'We will.'

The air shifted. Maggie sensed it, much like how a room reacts when its balance is disturbed.

Evelyn's smile tightened. 'Is this really necessary? People are already unsettled.'

'This is a homicide investigation,' Harris said. 'What people feel about it isn't my concern.'

Her gaze flicked to Maggie, sharp now. Calculating. Maggie met it without flinching.

'I want a meeting,' Evelyn said. 'This afternoon.'

Harris shook his head once. 'You can speak to a solicitor.'

Evelyn inhaled slowly, then nodded. 'Very well.'

She turned and walked away, posture rigid, control slipping just enough to show.

Harris watched her go. 'She knows.'

'Yes,' Maggie said. 'And she's afraid.'

'Of being arrested?'

'No,' Maggie replied. 'Of being exposed.'

Harris looked at her, then at the corridor Evelyn had disappeared down. 'Then let's make sure it happens properly.'

Maggie nodded. The pieces were no longer scattered. They were aligning, whether Evelyn wanted them to or not.

And there was no putting them back now.

***

The clerk didn't take long to crack. Harris hadn't even needed to push. The moment the preservation order went through, and access was locked down, the woman folded in on herself, her hands shaking as she tried to explain she'd only been following instructions. She sat in a small interview room at the back of the station, shoulders hunched, eyes fixed on the table as if looking up might make things worse.

'I didn't change anything important,' she said for the third time. 'I just moved files. Archived them properly.'

'After Arthur Bell died,' Harris said.

She swallowed. 'Yes.'

'And before the car was found.'

Her fingers twisted together. 'I didn't know about the car.'

Maggie stood to one side, silent, watching the way the clerk's words kept circling the same point without ever touching it. Fear made people careful, but it also made them sloppy.

'Who told you to move the files?' Harris asked.

The clerk hesitated, then shook her head. 'She didn't tell me what they were. Just that they were causing unnecessary confusion.'

'Who?' Harris repeated.

The clerk's voice dropped. 'Evelyn.'

The name landed quietly, and no one seemed surprised. That was the most revealing part.

'What files?' Harris asked.

'Land reclassification records,' the clerk said. 'Old ones. Backdated amendments. I was told they'd already been reviewed and approved years ago, but they were still popping up in search results because someone had flagged them.'

'Arthur,' Maggie said quietly.

The clerk nodded. 'Yes. He'd been asking for copies. Making notes. I thought he was just being thorough.'

'And after he died?' Harris asked.

'She said it would be best if the records were tidied up,' the clerk said. 'So the town could move forward.'

Maggie felt a familiar sense of cold clarity washing over her. Tidy—that word again. It reflected the same instinct that drove people to repeat the story of the accident, and the same desire to smooth out rough edges rather than examine them.

'What did those records show?' Harris asked.

The clerk hesitated again, then took a breath as if bracing herself. 'That land along the river—the block near the old causeway, it wasn't meant to be rezoned. Not when it was. There were flood risk assessments that should have stopped it.'

'But it went through,' Maggie said.

'Yes,' the clerk replied. 'After the reports were refiled. The risk classification was downgraded.'

Harris leaned forward slightly. 'And who benefited?'

The clerk's eyes flicked to Maggie, then back to the table. 'Evelyn. Her family trust bought it cheaply before the change. Sold portions later at a significant profit.'

Maggie pictured the fence posts she'd seen earlier, the boundary shifted just enough to matter. 'Arthur noticed.'

'Yes,' the clerk said. 'He asked why the original reports didn't match the final decision.'

'And that was a problem,' Harris said.

The clerk nodded, tears finally spilling over. 'I didn't know it would come to this.'

Harris straightened. 'You didn't kill anyone,' he said. 'But you helped hide how it happened.'

The clerk flinched. 'I never meant to….'

'I know,' Harris said. 'But intention doesn't undo consequence.'

Outside the interview room, Maggie stepped aside as Harris spoke quietly to another officer, arranging follow-up interviews and formal statements. The system was unravelling now, thread by thread, not because anyone was particularly brave, but because it had been built on convenience and silence.

Evelyn's phone rang before Harris finished issuing instructions. She stood in her office, one hand braced against the window, watching the street below as the call came through. Maggie saw her answer it, saw the moment her expression shifted, composure tightening into something brittle.

Evelyn hung up and turned as Maggie entered the doorway. 'You should leave,' Evelyn said. 'This isn't your place.'

Maggie didn't move. 'It's a public place.'

Evelyn's jaw set. 'You're enjoying this.'

'No,' Maggie replied. 'I enjoy the truth, and I want justice for Arthur.'

Evelyn laughed softly, a sound without humour. 'You think you understand how this town works.'

'I understand how you work,' Maggie said. 'You didn't trust anyone else to stop Arthur.'

Evelyn's eyes flickered—just once.

'You paid people to alter records,' Maggie continued. 'You relied on them to stay silent because it suited them. But when Arthur uncovered your deception and fraud, you couldn't pass the blame onto others to silence him permanently.'

Evelyn said nothing.

'You went yourself,' Maggie said. 'Because you believed you could control the outcome.'

Evelyn's voice was steady when she finally spoke. 'You don't have proof.'

'Maybe not yet,' Maggie agreed. 'But the car's been found. The autopsy confirms the injury. The records show motive. The rest is timing.'

Evelyn turned back to the window. 'He should have let it go.'

Silence stretched between them.

Harris stepped into the room, purposeful, folder under his arm. Evelyn watched him approach, then closed her eyes briefly, as if committing herself to a decision she'd already made.

Maggie stepped back, giving Harris space as he entered.

'Evelyn Crowe,' Harris said evenly. 'I'm placing you under arrest on suspicion of murder.'

Evelyn opened her eyes and met his gaze. 'On what grounds?'

'On grounds that will be made clear,' Harris replied. 'You have the right to remain silent.'

As Harris recited the caution, Maggie watched Evelyn carefully. Not for panic, not for anger, but for the moment, control finally slipped.

It came when Harris mentioned Arthur's name.

Just for a second, Evelyn's shoulders sagged before the mask was quickly back in place.

But it was too late. The system she'd built had turned against her, one careful piece at a time.

And Maggie knew, with the same quiet certainty she'd trusted all along, that there was no escaping what came next.

Evelyn didn't resist when Harris guided her toward the door. She gathered her handbag, smoothed her jacket, and walked with the measured composure of someone determined not to give the room what it wanted. If anyone watching expected spectacle, they were disappointed. There was none. Just the soft click of heels, the scrape of a chair as it was pushed back, and the quiet certainty of what had begun.

Maggie moved aside as they passed. Evelyn did not look at her this time. That, more than anything else, felt like confirmation of guilt.

Outside, the afternoon carried on as if nothing had happened. Cars moved along the street. Someone crossed with a coffee in hand. The world had not paused to acknowledge what was unfolding inside the council building, and it would not. Harris opened the back door of the police vehicle and waited while Evelyn stepped in. He shut it carefully, then turned to Maggie.

'This is where it gets serious,' he said. 'Interviews. Statements. Challenges.'

'I know,' Maggie replied.

He spoke briefly with another officer, giving instructions that would have effects throughout the day. Phones started ringing, files were requested, and those who thought they were on the sidelines would realise they were not.

When Harris was done, he walked back toward Maggie, lowering his voice. 'We've confirmed the access gate was unlocked using a council key assigned to Evelyn. That log adjustment was made from her office terminal.'

'And the car?' Maggie asked.

'Recovery found marks on the bank consistent with a controlled descent. Rope fibres too. Not from the river. From equipment.'

He paused. 'Someone planned it just enough to believe it would disappear.'

Maggie nodded. 'She trusted the river.'

'Yes,' Harris said. 'And she trusted the town to accept what it was told.'

They stood together for a moment, neither in a hurry to speak. The weight of the last week pressed in, not as exhaustion but as a settling. Maggie felt it in her shoulders, the release of tension she hadn't fully acknowledged she'd been carrying.

'I'll need you to help with one more thing,' Harris said. 'Arthur's notes. The missing pages.'

'They weren't missing by accident,' Maggie replied. 'They were carefully removed.'

'We need to leave nothing to chance. Evelyn is well-connected and respected. We need to make sure this sticks and the truth comes to light.'

Maggie nodded, and as Harris re-entered the building, while she remained outside, watching Evelyn's car being driven off by another officer. It felt important to witness it depart to feel not a sense of triumph, but a sense of finality.

She drove home slowly, taking streets she hadn't in days. The town appeared unchanged, with shopfronts open and people chatting. Nothing indicated the shift that had occurred beneath the surface. That realisation would come later, during retellings, in the awkward silences when familiar names were mentioned.

At home, Maggie set her bag down and went straight to the table by the window. The jigsaw she'd been working on sat half-complete, pieces clustered by colour and shape. She sat and fitted one into place, then another, the small click of cardboard against cardboard steadying her thoughts.

She hadn't solved this by instinct or luck. She'd done it the way she did everything else. Slowly and with care. She and Arthur had had more in common than she knew. Both had taken things slowly, being quiet yet sure, and both believed in uncovering the truth.

Her phone buzzed again. A message from Harris.

Forensics confirmed. Blood on the rock matches Arthur.

Maggie closed her eyes briefly, then replied with a simple thumbs-up emoji.

She returned to the puzzle, her fingers moving without urgency now. Outside, light shifted across the yard as the afternoon wore on. Somewhere, upstream, the river continued its work, reshaping its edges, carrying on without regard for what it had held or given up.

The town would change after this. It wouldn't happen all at once or loudly, but the sense of comfort from simple explanations was shattered, which was significant.

Maggie added another piece and leaned back, examining the emerging picture. It was almost complete now. Not perfect, but sufficiently whole to see.

For the first time since Arthur Bell was discovered by the river, Maggie felt confident that the whole truth would come out and he would receive some justice.

Chapter Nineteen

Maggie did not go to the library that morning. The decision seemed somewhat rebellious, though she knew it wasn't really. The library wasn't fragile; it didn't need her constant oversight to stay intact. The books would remain in place, just as they had been the previous day. The catalogue wouldn't fall apart. Well-constructed systems stay stable because they are solid, not because someone constantly monitors them. The focus now was not merely on maintaining order, but on understanding the reasons behind the rearrangement, so she went for a drive instead.

The route was familiar, one she had already envisioned multiple times, although she had never actually travelled it before. She avoided the river and the council chambers, which were crowded and noisy. Instead, she picked a quieter place, a place most people overlooked precisely because nothing important was meant to happen there.

The old planning annex was located behind the main council building, a small concrete structure that seemed like an afterthought. It was constructed years after the original offices became overcrowded and was never fully integrated into the daily activities of the site. Files that were no longer needed but couldn't be discarded were sent there. People used the space when they needed to work without interruptions or when they were meant to be somewhere else entirely.

Maggie parked across the road and remained in the car for a moment, hands resting lightly on the steering wheel as she watched the entrance. She was not waiting for anyone in particular. She was watching for repetition. For the small, ordinary habits that revealed themselves when people believed no one was paying attention.

She watched as the door opened twice. The first time, a young woman exited, carrying a box of archived folders, moving swiftly, her eyes fixed ahead and her posture leaning forward, clearly determined not to be delayed. The second time, a man emerged, paused briefly outside the door, as if contemplating whether to have a smoke. After a moment, he appeared to reconsider and re-entered. Maggie recognised him.

Over the years, he frequented the library often but never for books. It was always the public terminals he visited, usually during odd hours when the library was less crowded. He never borrowed anything, never stayed too long, and never asked questions that could leave a record. Once, he inquired with Maggie about the scanner, but never used it. On another occasion, he stood too close to the printer, watching a document emerge that wasn't his.

At the time, she had noticed, then moved on. Observation did not require accusation. Not everything needed a meaning assigned to it straight away, but now, she saw him clearly. She got out of the car and crossed the road at an unhurried pace. There was no advantage in rushing. People who believed themselves unseen tended to panic when approached calmly.

Inside, the annex smelled faintly of dust and toner. The lighting was harsher than in the main council building, fluorescent and unforgiving. Maggie followed the sound of a printer toward the back room, her footsteps measured, her presence unannounced.

He stood at a long table strewn with open folders. He was not reading them so much as checking them, cross-referencing dates, comparing stamps, running his finger along margins where something had once been written and later removed.

He looked up when he heard her.

A flicker crossed his face for a moment, but it was neither guilt nor fear. It was a calculation. He quickly regained composure, straightening up and offering a polite smile that did not reach his eyes.

'Maggie,' he said. 'Didn't expect to see you here.'

'I didn't expect to see you here either,' she replied. 'Not today.'

He adjusted his stance slightly. 'Just helping tidy things up.'

Maggie glanced at the folders. 'After the preservation order?'

His smile tightened. 'Some things still need sorting.'

'Not anymore,' Maggie said evenly. 'That window closed.'

He gave a light shrug. 'You'd be surprised how much gets missed.'

She stepped closer, just enough to read the file headings without touching them. They looked familiar. Too familiar. Land classifications. Historical amendments. Flood overlays. The same cluster Arthur had been circling before he died.

'You're not doing maintenance,' Maggie said. 'You're checking exposure.'

He let out a soft laugh. 'You always were imaginative.'

'No,' Maggie replied. 'I'm meticulous.'

That caused him to hesitate. She observed it in how he reevaluated her—no longer just as a librarian noticing details, but as someone who understood systems. This was the common mistake people made: believing libraries were solely about books. They overlooked that libraries were fundamentally about access.

'You didn't kill Arthur,' Maggie said, watching him closely. 'But you helped make his work disappear.'

This time, the laugh did not come. He turned back to the table and began stacking folders with unnecessary care. 'You're speculating.'

'I'm reconstructing,' Maggie said. 'You knew how to adjust timestamps without triggering alerts. You knew which files could be buried under routine without raising suspicion. And you panicked when the preservation order went through.'

He placed one folder down too hard. The sound cracked sharply through the room. 'You don't know what you're talking about.'

'I do,' Maggie said calmly. 'Because you didn't erase everything. You just made it harder to see. You assumed no one would take the time to look sideways.'

She reached into her bag and pulled out a single page. It wasn't a report or an accusation, just a comparison table she had assembled late last night. Original flood risk assessment dates, final rezoning approvals, and adjusted access logs, all aligned.

'You changed the sequence,' she said. 'But you didn't change the spacing. You didn't think anyone would notice the rhythm.'

He stared at the page, then looked away.

'Evelyn asked you to,' Maggie continued. 'Not directly at first. She framed it as protection. For the town. For development. For progress.'

'She didn't tell me anyone would die,' he said sharply.

'I know,' Maggie replied. 'If she had, you wouldn't be standing here.'

The words landed. She could see it in the slow drop of his shoulders, the release of something he had been holding up for too long.

'She said Arthur was causing trouble,' he said. 'That he was stirring things that had already been resolved.'

'And you believed her.'

'I believed the paperwork,' he said. 'The approvals were there. The signatures. Everything looked legitimate.'

'Because you helped make it look that way.'

He swallowed. 'I didn't think it mattered.'

'It mattered when Arthur noticed the gaps,' Maggie said. 'And it mattered when Evelyn realised she couldn't rely on systems anymore.'

He looked at her properly then. 'She did it

herself?'

Maggie didn't reply immediately, but she didn't have to. The truth was already lying between them.

'She didn't trust anyone else to complete it,' she finally said. 'And she trusted you to help clean up afterwards.'

Silence settled between them, heavy but contained. Somewhere behind them, the printer hummed and spat out a page no one moved to collect.

'They'll come for me,' he said finally, his voice low.

'They already have,' Maggie replied. 'You just don't know it yet.'

He closed his eyes for a moment, then nodded once, as if confirming something he had already accepted.

'I didn't change the land boundaries,' he said quietly. 'That was done before me. But I made sure no one could trace how.'

'That's enough,' Maggie said. 'And it's exactly what Harris needs.'

He looked at her again, resignation settling in. 'You're not police.'

'No,' Maggie agreed. 'That's why you talked.'

She stepped back, giving him space he no longer seemed to know what to do with.

'Stay here,' she said. 'Don't touch anything else.'

He did not argue. He stood where he was, hands resting on the table, surrounded by the evidence he had believed was safely buried.

Maggie left the annex and stepped back into the light, already reaching for her phone. Harris answered on the second ring.

'I've got him,' she said. 'And he's ready to talk.'

Harris did not keep her waiting. Maggie

remained outside the annex, phone in hand, as she watched his vehicle drive in at the end of the lane. The air carried a faint metallic scent that seemed to linger around council buildings despite frequent cleaning. Harris parked smoothly, got out, and exchanged a look that conveyed he now trusted her instincts, even if the rest of the town didn't.

'You sure?' he asked.

'Yes,' Maggie replied. 'He's inside. He hasn't bolted. And he hasn't had time to tidy the mess he's been making.'

Harris's mouth tightened, not with irritation but focus. 'Good.'

Two uniformed officers followed him in. Maggie noticed, with quiet approval, that Harris did not enter loudly. He was not looking for a scene. He was looking for leverage.

They proceeded along the corridor in silence, their footsteps muffled on the linoleum.

Maggie trailed slightly behind Harris, not out of deference but to maintain her perspective, observing the subtle shifts that occur first when someone chooses to cooperate or resist.

In the back room, the man was still at the table. His hands were placed carefully beside the folders, as if he had decided the safest approach was to appear harmless. The page in the printer tray had curled at the edges.

Harris took him in without blinking. 'Name.'

The man swallowed. 'Gareth.'

'Gareth what?' Harris asked.

He hesitated, then gave his surname. Harris nodded once, filing it away, then gestured toward the table. 'Step away from the documents.'

Gareth complied without argument. That, in itself, said plenty. People who believed they had a story strong enough to protect them usually tried it first.

Harris scanned the folders without touching them. 'You're aware there's a preservation order.'

'Yes,' Gareth said quickly. 'I wasn't changing anything. I was checking what had already been archived.'

'Why?' Harris asked.

Gareth's eyes flicked to Maggie, then back to Harris. 'Because people keep misunderstanding things. It's become messy.'

Maggie heard the phrasing and almost smiled. It was the same instinct she had seen all over town, just dressed differently. Not truth or lies. Neatness or mess.

Harris turned slightly and met Maggie's eyes. 'You want to tell me what you told her?'

Gareth's face tightened. 'I didn't—'

Harris lifted a hand. Not threatening. Final. 'Don't waste my time. Maggie didn't ring me because you were chatting about the weather.'

The silence that followed was heavy.

Maggie moved forward, not into Gareth's space but into his line of sight, forcing the acknowledgment of her presence. 'You know the difference between maintenance and concealment,' she said. 'And you know you crossed it.'

Gareth's jaw worked. He looked down, then up again, as if choosing which kind of trouble he wanted. 'I didn't kill anyone.'

'No,' Maggie said steadily. 'But you helped make it look like no one did.'

Harris's voice remained calm, which somehow made it worse. 'Start from the beginning.'

Gareth drew a breath. 'It started years ago.'

Harris tilted his head slightly. 'Not years. Start from the moment you were instructed to touch anything tied to Arthur Bell.'

Gareth swallowed. 'After he died.'

' Who instructed you?' Harris asked.

'It wasn't like that,' Gareth said quickly. 'Not at first. It wasn't direct.'

'I'll ask again,' Harris said. 'Who instructed you?'

Gareth exhaled hard. 'Evelyn.'

The name appeared once more, weighty and unmistakable. Maggie felt no satisfaction, only a sense of clarity.

Harris nodded once. 'What did she want you to do?'

'She said Arthur was confusing things,' Gareth replied. 'That he didn't understand context. That he was pulling out old drafts and preliminary reports and treating them as decisions.'

Maggie narrowed her eyes. It was the kind of justification that made wrongdoing seem acceptable.

'And you believed her,' she said.

'I believed the approvals,' Gareth replied. 'The signatures were there. Everything looked legitimate.'

'What files?' Harris asked.

Gareth glanced at the table. 'Flood overlays. Risk assessments. Land classification changes near the river corridor. The block near the old causeway. And a few adjacent lots that were meant to stay non-developable.'

Maggie's mental map clicked into place. Fence posts. Boundaries. Silent shifts that impacted much more than just paper.

'And what did Evelyn want?' Harris asked.

Gareth hesitated. 'She wanted it to be clean.'

Maggie flicked a glance at Harris. He heard it too. That word always surfaced. Clean.

As if language could erase consequences.

'She said the town needed to move on,' Gareth continued. 'That people wouldn't understand the technical side. That if Arthur kept talking about inconsistencies, it would turn into rumours.'

'So, you altered access logs,' Harris said.

'Not like forging,' Gareth protested. 'I adjusted things. Refiled. Made archived drafts harder to find. The final approvals were still there.'

'You backdated the path,' Maggie said.

Gareth's eyes snapped to her. 'I didn't backdate approvals.'

'You backdated how people would reach the truth,' Maggie replied. 'Same outcome.'

Harris nodded. 'What else?'

Gareth clasped his hands tightly. 'There was a volume of council minutes. Physical. It couldn't be hidden digitally. Evelyn asked me to retrieve it.'

Maggie felt a small jolt of confirmation. The missing volume. The altered due date. 'You took it,' she said.

'I was told it had sensitive personal details,' Gareth replied. 'Names. It wasn't meant for general access.'

'And where is it now?' Harris asked.

'Not here.'

'Where?'

Gareth's eyes flicked toward the corridor. 'Her office. Locked cabinet. She said she'd return it once everything settled down.'

Harris's jaw tightened. 'Everything was never going to settle down. Not after a man died.'

'I didn't know she killed him,' Gareth said quickly.

Maggie watched him carefully. She believed that much. What she also believed was that he had suspected afterwards and chosen not to look too closely.

'You knew something was wrong,' Maggie said. 'Because you rushed. You didn't do it the way you do real work.'

'She called me the night after he was found,' Gareth said.

'What did she say?' Harris asked.

'That the police were classifying it as natural. That it would all be fine if no one stirred it up. And then she said Arthur's name like it was an inconvenience.'

'And you complied,' Maggie said.

'I didn't want to think,' Gareth admitted.

Harris stepped forward. 'You understand you interfered with a homicide investigation.'

'I didn't touch evidence,' Gareth said weakly.

'You touched the record trail that makes motive visible,' Harris replied. 'That counts.'

Gareth's breathing grew shallow.

'You can still do one useful thing,' Maggie said. 'Tell us who else helped.'

'It wasn't organised,' Gareth said. 'Just favours.'

'Names,' Harris said.

An IT contractor, a retired planning officer, and a records worker who misplaced boxes—gradually, the truth emerged.

Harris turned to one of the officers. 'Secure the room. Photograph everything. I want a warrant for Evelyn's office cabinet immediately.'

Gareth's face crumpled. 'She'll blame me.'

'She's been blaming others her whole life,' Maggie said. 'That's why she lasted this long.'

Harris faced Gareth. 'You're under arrest.'

The words hit hard, and Gareth steadied himself by bracing against the table.

As Harris instructed the officer to read the caution, Maggie looked at the folders again. Paper had never been harmless. It controlled land, money, and power. And now it was controlling Evelyn.

Maggie stepped into the corridor as Harris finished up. Her phone buzzed.

Stop. You don't know what you're doing.

No name. Private Number.

She slipped the phone back into her pocket without replying. She did not feel frightened. She felt finished with being polite.

Harris did not look back as he led Gareth down the corridor. Maggie stayed where she was, leaning lightly against the wall as the building adjusted around what had just broken open. Council buildings always did. Sounds sharpened. Movements became careful.

Her phone vibrated again.

You're making a mistake.

She left it unanswered.

Harris returned a few minutes later, jacket off, sleeves rolled. 'He's talking,' he said. 'Enough.'

'We've got officers heading to Evelyn's office,' he added. 'Cabinet. Computer. Personal files.'

'And the council minutes volume?' Maggie asked.

'Found,' Harris said. 'False backing.'

They walked toward the exit together. Outside, late afternoon light stretched across the pavement.

'There's something I want your take on,' Harris said. 'Why Evelyn did it herself.'

'Because Arthur wasn't loud,' Maggie said. 'He just kept looking.'

'And she couldn't intimidate him,' Harris said.

'Or buy him,' Maggie replied.

Harris nodded. 'And she doesn't trust people when it matters.'

'She only trusts systems she controls,' Maggie said. 'Until someone slips through.'

Harris unlocked his vehicle. 'I'm glad you didn't walk away.'

'So am I,' Maggie said.

She drove home via the river, slowing as the road curved close enough to see the water through the trees. It moved steadily, carrying what it carried, holding what it held.

At home, she went straight to the jigsaw by the window. Not many pieces remained. She fitted one into place, then another, without hurry.

Her phone buzzed.

We found the ledger. It's worse than we thought. I'll explain tomorrow.

She placed one more piece and leaned back. Not quite complete. Not perfect. Yet.

Outside, the light dimmed as the river carried on its course. Arthur had not let it, and she hadn't either. Now, neither would the truth.

Chapter Twenty

Maggie had a restless night and woke up early, as she often did when her mind fixated on a nearly resolved problem. The house was silent in that faint pre-dawn hour, making every small sound seem exaggerated. She stayed still for a moment, listening, then realised sleep wouldn't return and swung her legs out of bed.

The kettle clicked on in the kitchen. Outside, the sky was faint and uncertain, still awaiting the day's full arrival. Maggie stood at the bench, hands wrapped around her mug once it was filled, letting the heat anchor her. The rush of adrenaline from the past few days had faded, replaced by a calmer determination. It wasn't relief or satisfaction, but a clear sense of resolve.

Evelyn was in custody. That much was done. But the truth wasn't finished yet, and Maggie knew better than to assume it would simply surface on its own. People like Evelyn didn't act alone, and they didn't fall quietly. They relied on systems, on habits, on the assumption that everyone else would rather keep things comfortable than ask difficult questions.

After a quick breakfast of tea and toast with her husband, kissed him and reached for her bag. There were still loose ends, and she intended to pull them tight.

The police station was already awake when she arrived. Not busy, exactly, but alert. Phones rang and stopped ringing. Officers moved with purpose rather than urgency. Harris stood near the front desk, jacket off, sleeves rolled, a folder open in his hands. He looked up as she entered.

'I was hoping you'd come in,' he said.

'I wasn't going to stay home,' Maggie replied. 'Not today.'

He nodded once, understanding more than he said. 'We've had developments overnight.'

'Good ones?' she asked.

'Clarifying ones,' Harris said. 'Which, at this stage, is the same thing.'

He guided her down the corridor into a small interview room that had a faint scent of disinfectant and old coffee. The folder he was carrying was placed on the table between them.

'We've been reconstructing timelines,' he said. 'Movements. Access. Who was where, and when.'

'And?' Maggie prompted.

'And there's a gap,' Harris said. 'A deliberate one.'

He opened the folder and slid a page to

her. It wasn't dramatic, no bold headings or clear conclusions, just timestamps and names arranged neatly. Maggie read it once, then again.

'This window,' she said, tapping the page lightly. 'Late evening. After Arthur left the library.'

'Yes,' Harris replied. 'That's when records were accessed remotely. Not altered. Viewed.'

'Someone checking what he'd already found,' Maggie said.

'Exactly.'

She leaned back in her chair, the pieces aligning in her mind without effort now. 'Evelyn wouldn't have done that herself.'

'No,' Harris agreed. 'Too obvious. Too traceable.'

'But she'd want to know how much trouble she was in,' Maggie said. 'What Arthur knew. What he might have copied.'

Harris watched her carefully. 'You're thinking there's someone else.'

'I'm thinking there has always been someone else,' Maggie said. 'She didn't get where she is by doing everything with her own hands.'

Harris was quiet for a moment. 'We've identified three people with the level of access needed to view those records at that time. Two have alibis that hold up.'

'And the third?' Maggie asked.

Harris didn't answer immediately. Instead, he closed the folder and met her gaze. 'That's where you come in.'

Maggie felt the familiar tightening in her chest, not fear but focus. 'You want me to talk to them.'

'I want you to notice what we might miss,' Harris said. 'You're not bound by procedure. And they won't see you coming.'

Maggie considered that, then nodded. 'All right. Who is it?'

Harris gave her a name. Not one she'd been expecting, but not a stranger either. Someone who sat just far enough from the centre of things to avoid attention. Someone who'd always seemed helpful. Available. Reliable.

'Of course,' Maggie said quietly – the realisation dawning.

Harris exhaled. 'You see it too.'

'Yes,' she replied. 'I think I always have. I just didn't know what I was looking at yet.'

Harris pushed back his chair and stood. 'I'll make sure we're close if this goes sideways.'

'It won't,' Maggie said, standing as well. 'Not today.'

She left the station with the name echoing in her thoughts, not with anger but with a clear-eyed understanding of how easily trust could be used as cover. The town hadn't been fooled by one person. It had been managed by several, each doing their small part and telling themselves it wasn't their responsibility to question the whole. That was the lie Maggie intended to dismantle.

She didn't go straight to confront anyone. Instead, she walked, letting the movement settle her thoughts. Past the shops. Past the places where people would soon start talking in lower voices, where familiar names would begin to carry a different weight. She passed the library without stopping, feeling its presence like a quiet companion rather than a destination.

By the time she turned toward her next stop, she knew exactly what she was going to say—and, more importantly, what to listen for—since people rarely confessed when accused. However, they almost always let their true selves show when they thought they were still being understood.

She didn't like arriving too close when she didn't know what she might find. It gave her a moment to settle her thoughts, to let her breathing even out before she stepped into someone else's space. The afternoon had thinned into that quiet stretch where most people were still at work or pretending to be, the town held in a lull that felt deceptively calm.

The building looked unchanged. That was the first thing she noticed. Same peeling paint at the corner of the verandah. Same crooked pot plant beside the door, dry despite the rain earlier in the week. It was the kind of place people stopped seeing once they'd passed it enough times. Maggie didn't knock straight away.

She positioned herself beside the door, listening. Not for voices — she wasn't anticipating any — but for signs of movement, subtle clues that someone was present and alert instead of away. When no sounds came, she knocked once, firmly, and then waited.

No answer.

She knocked again, a fraction louder this time, and stepped back.

The door opened on the third knock.

He didn't look surprised to see her. That, more than anything else, told her she'd been right to come.

'Can I help you?' he said, though his eyes had already moved past her, scanning the street behind.

'I won't take long,' Maggie replied. She kept her tone neutral, unthreatening. 'I just wanted to ask you a few questions.'

He hesitated, and Maggie waited. She knew that silence, when used effectively, can be more powerful than pressure. At last, he moved aside.

Inside, the place had a faint aroma of stale coffee and fresh paper. Not old paper, but recent, with files frequently moved. The disorder seemed driven by habit rather than concern. Maggie observed this quickly: the stack of folders on the table, the laptop still open, and his keys casually dropped beside it.

'I should probably have a solicitor,' he said, too late to sound convincing.

'I'm not here in any official capacity,' Maggie replied. 'I'm here because things don't add up, and I think you know that.'

He didn't answer. He sat instead, hands clasped together, elbows on his knees. A man preparing to endure something rather than stop it.

'You didn't mean to get involved,' Maggie continued. 'None of this started that way.'

His jaw tightened.

'You were asked to make changes,' she

said. 'Small ones. Adjustments that didn't feel like harm because they were framed as corrections. Tidying. Making things consistent.'

He looked up at her then. Just briefly. 'That's how she explained it,' he said.

Maggie nodded.

She didn't sit down. Instead, she remained in place, grounded and steady. 'The issue is, once Arthur noticed, it was no longer about paperwork.'

He exhaled slowly, a sound caught somewhere between frustration and resignation. 'He wouldn't let it go.'

'No,' Maggie agreed. 'He wasn't that kind of man.'

Silence settled between them again. This time, it felt heavier.

'You didn't plan for him to die,' Maggie said. 'But you helped after. You adjusted access logs. You delayed queries. You told yourself it was already done, that nothing you did changed the outcome.'

His shoulders sagged. Just a little.

'I didn't know she was going to hurt him,' he said. 'I swear I didn't.'

'I believe you,' Maggie said. And she did. 'But you knew enough afterwards to realise what you were protecting.'

He rubbed his face with both hands, dragging them down slowly. 'She said the river would take care of it.'

Maggie felt the familiar cold settle into place. 'And you believed her.'

'I wanted to,' he replied.

She let that sit. People often mistook wanting something to be true for proof.

'You're not the only one who made that mistake,' Maggie said. 'But now it's too late to pretend it didn't matter.'

He looked up at her then, properly. 'What

happens now?'

'That depends,' Maggie said gently, 'on whether you keep choosing silence.'

Outside, a car passed. Somewhere nearby, a door slammed. Life continuing, indifferent. Maggie shifted her weight slightly. 'Senior Constable Harris already knows someone helped her. He just doesn't know how far it went yet.'

His breath hitched.

'I came because I thought you'd want the chance to tell the truth before he asks.'

She didn't say arrest. She didn't need to.

He closed his eyes. When he spoke again, his voice was quieter. 'I can't fix what I did.'

'No,' Maggie said. 'But you can stop it spreading any further.' She waited, and this time, she knew he would talk.

He didn't start at the beginning. People never did when they were finally telling the truth. They started where it hurt the most.

'I didn't think it would go as far as it did,' he said. 'That's the part I keep circling back to.'

Maggie stayed where she was, hands loose at her sides, her body open but grounded. She'd learned not to rush this moment. Once someone crossed the line into honesty, the worst thing you could do was interrupt the shape of it.

'She'd been asking for years,' he continued. 'Not directly. Never in writing. Just… comments. Observations. Things she said aloud as if she were thinking them through. 'That classification never made sense.' 'That report doesn't reflect how the land actually behaves.' Stuff like that.'

'And you listened,' Maggie said.

'Yes.' He gave a short, humourless laugh. 'Because she was persuasive. And because she was right often enough that it felt reasonable to trust her when she said something needed correcting.'

Maggie nodded once. She could see it clearly. The slow slide. The way authority softened resistance when it arrived dressed as confidence rather than force.

'She knew the system better than most,' he said. 'Not the technical side. The people side. She knew who hated paperwork, who hated conflict, who just wanted things neat and final.'

'And Arthur didn't fit,' Maggie said.

'No,' he agreed. 'Arthur asked questions. He didn't accept 'that's how it's always been done' as an answer. And he remembered things other people had forgotten.'

He rubbed his thumb along the edge of the table, back and forth, as if calming himself with the texture. 'When he started requesting old flood assessments, she noticed straight away. She asked me if he'd always been that thorough.' Maggie listened without responding.

'She asked me to move some files,' he went on. 'Just re-archive them. Change the search flags so they didn't come up unless someone knew exactly what to look for. She said it was temporary. That it would stop unnecessary confusion.'

'After Arthur died,' Maggie said quietly.

He swallowed. 'Yes.'

That was the moment. Maggie felt it fall into place, the way a final piece always did when you stopped trying to force it and let it find its own edge.

'You knew then,' she said. 'That this wasn't about efficiency anymore.'

'I knew it wasn't clean,' he replied. 'I didn't know she'd done it herself. I thought… I thought it was an accident that she was trying to manage.'

Maggie tilted her head slightly. 'But you helped anyway.'

'Yes.'

'She said the river would make it simpler,' he added. 'That it always did. That once things passed through it, people stopped asking questions.'

Maggie felt the familiar tightening in her chest, not anger exactly, but something colder. 'She trusted the river,' she said.

'And the town,' he replied. 'She trusted people to accept what felt easiest.'

They sat with that for a moment until finally, Maggie spoke. 'You adjusted the access logs.'

'Yes.'

'And the service gate.'

'Yes.'

'You made it look as though routine work had happened later than it actually did.'

He nodded. 'So no one would question how the car got close enough to the bank.'

Maggie exhaled slowly. There it was. The thing that had bothered her since the beginning, now named properly.

'You didn't touch the car itself,' she said.

'No,' he replied quickly. 'I never went near it. That part was already done.'

'But you helped clear the path,' Maggie said.

'Yes.'

Outside, a dog barked. Somewhere down the street, someone laughed. The sound felt jarringly ordinary.

'When she realised Arthur wasn't going to stop,' Maggie said, 'she didn't trust anyone else to handle it.'

He shook his head. 'She said she couldn't risk someone panicking. Or talking. Or leaving something behind.'

'And she believed she wouldn't,' Maggie said.

'She believed she could control it,' he replied. 'Right up to the end.'

Maggie looked at him properly then. 'You need to tell Senior Constable Harris exactly what you've told me.'

He nodded, resignation settling in fully now. 'I will.'

She didn't offer comfort. She didn't offer reassurance. This wasn't the moment for either. She stepped back slightly. 'I'm going to step outside and make a call.'

He didn't try to stop her. He looked defeated, but like a weight had been lifted now that it was all out in the open. He let out a heavy sigh.

Maggie walked out into the late afternoon and pulled her phone from her pocket. Harris answered straight away.

'I've got it,' she said. 'He's ready to talk. Full statement. Access logs, gate timing, and file adjustments. He confirms Evelyn directed it all.'

Harris exhaled audibly. 'Good job, Maggie. We might make a real detective out of you yet.'

Maggie smiled at that. 'Not likely. She acted alone when it mattered, but she didn't do it without help afterwards.'

'That matches what we've got,' Harris said. 'I'm on my way.'

Maggie ended the call and stood for a moment longer, letting the air steady her. When she went back inside, the man was sitting exactly where she'd left him, hands folded now instead of clenched.

'She always said she was fixing things,' he said quietly.

Maggie met his gaze. 'Some people confuse fixing with erasing.'

Not long after, Harris arrived.

He didn't come in with noise or authority. He stepped into the room as if he belonged there, calm and precise, the way he always was when things finally made sense.

'I'll take it from here,' he said to Maggie. She nodded and stepped back, listening as the man began again, this time with a recorder on the table between them. The words came more easily now. Once spoken aloud, they didn't need protecting.

Maggie left before it was finished.

Outside, the light had shifted. The street looked no different than it had an hour earlier, but she felt the change anyway, the quiet release that came when something long-held finally loosened. She walked back to her car without hurry.

This part was done. There was still the aftermath ahead. Statements. Court dates. Consequences that would ripple outward in ways no one could fully predict. But the truth itself was no longer fragile. It didn't need guarding anymore.

As she drove away, Maggie didn't look back.

Chapter Twenty-One

The next morning, Maggie didn't go to work at the library. She knew it would all run perfectly smoothly without her, and so she had taken a few days' leave.

She had a destination in mind, but first, she just wanted to take a quiet drive, letting the roads carry her where they always had, through streets that looked no different than they had a week earlier. Shops were open, and cars were moving along the road. Someone stood outside the bakery with a coffee balanced on the roof of their car while they searched for keys in a bag. The world did not rearrange itself around the truth simply because it had finally been spoken aloud.

That was one of the things Maggie

understood better now than she had at the beginning. Justice did not arrive with noise, just with paperwork, altered routines, and people discovering that decisions they'd made casually would follow them longer than they'd expected.

She parked near the river but did not get out straight away. The water moved as it always did, surface broken by light and shadow, current steady where it narrowed, slower where it widened. It looked harmless as always. Maggie rested her hands on the steering wheel and watched it without sentiment, without accusation.

Arthur had been right about the land and about the records. And he had been right to keep going when it would have been easier to stop. Arthur had believed in uncovering the truth just as Maggie did.

She started the car again and drove on.

By the time she reached the council

building, the mood had shifted.

Not visibly, but if you knew how to read a space, you could feel it. Doors were closed that were usually open, conversations were hushed, and people moved with a kind of care that hadn't been there before, as if everyone had suddenly become aware that their actions left traces whether they intended them to or not.

Maggie walked through the foyer without announcing herself. She wasn't there to confront anyone, just to observe.

A notice had already been taped to the glass beside reception announcing temporary suspension of all development applications affecting flood-adjacent land with an independent review pending. The wording was neutral and professional. But the effect was immediate.

A councillor passed Maggie in the corridor and nodded, not the automatic greeting she'd received for years, but something more deliberate. Acknowledging, without saying anything at all, that things had changed. Maggie kept walking.

In the records office, the filing cabinets stood open. Boxes sat on tables. The air smelled of paper and dust, disturbed after years of being left alone. Two staff members worked quietly, gloves on, sorting documents into labelled stacks.

One looked up when Maggie appeared and hesitated.

'Morning,' Maggie said, neutral as ever.

The woman nodded. 'We're… reorganising.'

'I can see that,' Maggie replied.

The woman swallowed and went back to her work.

Maggie didn't stay. She didn't need to ask questions. The work was happening. That was enough.

Outside, she nearly ran into Harris as he stepped out of a meeting room, folder tucked under his arm.

'There you are,' he said, not surprised. 'I figured you'd come through.'

'I wanted to see it,' Maggie replied. 'The practical side of it.'

He nodded. 'It's started.'

They moved together toward the quieter end of the building, stopping near a window that looked out over the car park.

'The statement held,' Harris said. 'He confirmed everything again this morning. Names. Dates. Processes. Where the pressure came from and how it was applied.'

'And Evelyn?' Maggie asked.

'She hasn't said much,' Harris replied. 'But she hasn't denied it either.'

That told Maggie more than a speech ever

could.

Harris continued, 'Her solicitor requested a delay on the formal interview. Standard. But the evidence doesn't rely on her cooperation.'

'No,' Maggie agreed. 'It never did.'

Harris watched her for a moment. 'You don't seem surprised.'

'I stopped being surprised days ago,' Maggie said. 'What matters now is what holds.'

'It will,' Harris said. 'The paper trail is solid. The flood reports alone are enough to undo the rezoning. The financial records do the rest.'

'And the people who helped?' Maggie asked.

'Consequences,' Harris said simply. 'Different scales. Different outcomes. But no one's walking away untouched.'

Maggie nodded.

'That's as it should be.'

They stood there in silence for a moment, not uncomfortable, not companionable either. Just two people acknowledging that a line had been crossed and could not be uncrossed.

'I'll step back now,' Maggie said eventually.

Harris looked at her. 'You already have.'

'Yes,' she replied. 'But I wanted to say it out loud.'

He gave a small nod. 'Fair.'

Maggie went home after that.

Not because there was nothing left to do, but because her part was finished.

She dropped her bag on the chair by the door and stood in the kitchen for a moment, noticing things she hadn't paid attention to in days. A cup left by the sink. A thin layer of dust on the windowsill. The ordinary markers of a life that hadn't paused just because she had.

She made tea and carried it to the table by

the window.

The jigsaw sat where she'd left it, pieces grouped carefully, most of the picture already formed. She sat and fitted two pieces together without thinking, then stopped, studying the shape that remained.

This was the part she liked best.

Not the beginning, when everything was scattered.

Not the end, when there was nothing left to solve.

The middle, where clarity arrived not all at once, but steadily.

She worked for a while without checking the time.

Later that afternoon, her phone rang.

Harris again.

'They've formally reinstated the original flood classification,' he said. 'Effective immediately.'

Maggie closed her eyes briefly. 'Arthur would have liked that.'

'Yes,' Harris agreed. 'I think he would have.'

'There'll be appeals,' Maggie said.

'Of course,' Harris replied. 'But the foundation's gone. Without the altered reports, there's nothing to stand on.'

'And the land?' Maggie asked.

'Back where it should have been all along,' Harris said. 'Protected.'

Maggie smiled faintly.

'Good,' she said.

Harris hesitated, then added, 'There'll be an inquest component as well. Process review. System failures.'

'As there should be,' Maggie replied.

He exhaled. 'You don't want to be involved.'

'No,' Maggie said. 'I don't.'

'That's what I thought,' Harris replied. 'I'll keep you updated. Officially.'

She thanked him and ended the call.

In the days that followed, Maggie watched the consequences unfold without stepping into them.

Not from a distance exactly — she still lived here, still walked the same streets — but with intention.

A notice appeared on the library board acknowledging Arthur Bell's contribution to the local history archive. Simple. Accurate. No embellishment. Maggie approved it without comment.

A development proposal was withdrawn quietly. Another stalled. A third was returned with a request for additional assessments that everyone knew would not come back favourably.

People talked, of course.

But not to Maggie.

And that, she understood, was a sign of respect rather than exclusion.

They knew she'd seen enough.

One evening, she walked the river path again.

The track was quieter than usual. A couple passed her with a dog on a loose lead. Someone sat on a bench, looking out over the water without any obvious purpose.

Maggie paused near the bend where the car had been recovered.

The bank bore faint marks still, lines in the mud that rain would eventually soften. Nothing dramatic. Nothing that demanded attention.

She stood for a moment, then turned away.

She had done what Arthur would have done, given the chance.

That was enough.

Back home, she finished the jigsaw.

The last piece clicked into place with a sound she felt more than heard. She leaned back and looked at the completed picture without pride.

It wasn't perfect. A corner piece was slightly warped. The image itself wasn't especially beautiful.

But it was whole.

Maggie cleared the table carefully, returning the pieces to the box one section at a time. When she finished, she closed the lid and slid it onto the shelf.

There would be another puzzle soon enough.

Later that night, as she turned off the light, Maggie thought briefly of Evelyn.

With understanding.

Control, she knew now, wasn't power.

It was fear wearing a better suit.

And fear always left fingerprints, no

matter how carefully someone tried to wipe them away.

Maggie slept.

Chapter Twenty-Two

Maggie did not wake with urgency anymore.

That, more than anything else, told her the work was finished.

She woke at her usual time, before the alarm, but without the sharp edge that had carried her through the past weeks. Her mind moved slowly at first, not circling, not testing connections, not reaching for what might still be missing. The house felt like itself again. Familiar sounds. Familiar light through the curtains. The steady, unremarkable beginning of a day that did not require her to solve anything.

Martin was already up. She could hear him in the kitchen, moving with the quiet confidence of someone who knew where everything belonged without thinking about it. The kettle clicked off. A cupboard closed. He didn't call out to her. He never did. He trusted her to arrive when she was ready.

She lay still for a moment longer, not because she needed to, but because she could.

When she got up, dressed, and joined him, he handed her a mug without comment. Tea, the way she liked it. No question. No check-in disguised as casual conversation. Just the small, intimate understanding of two people who had learned when to speak and when not to.

'You working today?' he asked, eventually.

'Yes,' Maggie said. 'Normal hours.'

He nodded. 'I'll be in the garden this afternoon.'

'Good,' she said.

That was the extent of it. No discussion of Evelyn. No speculation about what would happen next. No recapping of what had already been decided by evidence and time. The case had taken up enough space. Neither of them was interested in letting it stretch further than necessary.

Outside, the morning was cool and clear. Maggie drove to the library along roads she hadn't avoided in days, past corners that had once pulled her attention inward. The town looked the same. That was expected. Change here never arrived loudly. It crept in sideways, through notices and absences and the quiet rearranging of routines.

The first sign came before she even reached the library.

A council notice had been pinned to the board outside the general store. Temporary appointments. An interim administrator. A meeting postponed until further notice. Nothing explanatory. Nothing emotional. Just information presented cleanly, as if clarity alone might restore order.

Inside the library, the air was cool and familiar. The smell of paper and dust and quiet work. Maggie unlocked the doors and went about the morning routine. Lights on. Computer terminals checked. The return chute emptied.

Arthur's desk had been cleared.

Not stripped, not erased, just reset. The drawers were empty. The surface wiped clean. The chair pushed in neatly. The space no longer belonged to anyone, and Maggie felt the absence without needing to dwell on it. Some things did not require ceremony to be acknowledged.

She opened the day's mail and sorted it without thought. Book requests. Notices. A letter from the state library confirming receipt of archived material Arthur had flagged weeks earlier. She placed it carefully in a folder and labelled it in his neat, precise style.

That felt right.

Mid-morning, Harris came in.

Not in uniform. Not officially. Just Harris, moving through the library as he always had, respectfully, as if the space demanded it. He didn't stop at the desk. He didn't lower his voice. He simply came to stand beside her as she reshelved returned books.

'It's done,' he said.

She didn't look at him. 'All of it?'

'Yes.'

Charges formalised. Statements logged. The accomplice's cooperation was documented fully. Financial trails mapped and verified. The land transactions were flagged for review beyond this town, now that the pattern had been exposed.

'Good,' Maggie said.

Harris waited a moment. 'You won't be needed anymore.'

'I know.'

He nodded. There was no gratitude in his expression, no attempt to wrap this in something larger than it was. Just acknowledgement.

'You did your part,' he said. 'Quietly. Properly.'

She slid a book into place and straightened. 'So did Arthur.'

'Yes,' Harris agreed. 'He did.'

He didn't stay long. That wasn't his way. He left the same way he'd come in, without marking the moment.

The rest of the day unfolded without incident.

People came and went. Books were borrowed. Questions were asked and answered. A child sat cross-legged in the corner and read until his mother called him away. Maggie moved through it all with ease, aware of the steady hum of normality returning.

By afternoon, the garden at home was visible from the library windows, and Martin bent over a row of newly turned soil. She watched him for a moment, then returned to her work.

This was what justice looked like here.

Not applause.

Not relief.

Not the satisfaction of being right.

Just things returning to their proper order.

When she closed the library that evening, she did so without ceremony. She turned the key, checked the handle, and walked to her car. The light had softened, the day settling into evening without drama.

At home, Martin was washing his hands at the sink when she came in.

'Dinner in twenty,' he said.

She nodded. 'I'll change.'

They ate together at the table, the way they always had. Simple food. Easy conversation. He told her about a stubborn root he'd finally given up on. She told him about a reader who'd returned the wrong book twice and apologised both times as if it were a personal failing.

Later, when the dishes were done and the house had settled again, Maggie brought out the jigsaw.

Only a few pieces remained now.

She didn't rush them.

She fitted one into place, then another, watching the picture come together without surprise. When the final piece clicked in, she didn't pause or admire it for long. Completion didn't need witnessing.

She stood, stretched slightly, and turned out the light.

Outside, the river moved as it always had.

Not as an answer.

Not as a symbol.

Just water finding its way forward.

And Maggie, for the first time in a long while, slept through the night.

Epilogue

The library was quiet in the way Maggie liked best — not empty, not hushed by rule, but settled. The kind of quiet that came from people knowing where they were and what they needed from the space.

She stood behind the desk for a moment before sitting, her hand resting on the worn timber surface, grounding herself in the familiar texture. The desk had belonged to Arthur once. Not officially. Just by habit. By presence. He'd favoured the corner nearest the reference shelves, close enough to reach what he needed without standing, far enough from the door that he could observe who came and went without feeling watched himself.

It still bore the faint scratches from his pen, the shallow groove where he'd tapped absentmindedly when thinking. Maggie had noticed them early on and left them untouched. They weren't damage. They were history.

The case was over.

Not finished—that would be much longer—but over in the way that mattered to her. Charges had been laid. Statements signed. The mechanisms that had allowed everything to happen had been dragged into the light and dismantled piece by piece. There were still consequences unfolding, but they were no longer hers to carry.

She'd returned to work three days after everything formally closed.

Harris had suggested she take more time. Martin had too, in his careful way, offering without insisting. Maggie had considered it, then declined. Routine mattered to her. The familiar rhythm of the library gave her something to step back into that wasn't shaped by questions or vigilance.

The first day back, she'd moved slowly through the shelves, reordering returns, straightening spines, listening to the ordinary sounds of people using the space as intended. It had felt almost unreal, the absence of tension. Like standing in a room after a storm had passed, noticing what was still intact.

Now, weeks later, that sense of unreality had faded.

This was simply how things were again.

A woman approached the desk with a stack of books held carefully against her chest. Maggie recognised her immediately — a regular, though they'd never spoken beyond polite exchanges.

'Morning,' Maggie said.

'Morning,' the woman replied, then

hesitated. 'I just wanted to say… thank you.'

Maggie met her eyes. 'For?'

'For keeping this place steady,' the woman said. 'Through all of it.'

Maggie nodded, accepting the words without deflecting them. 'That's what it's here for.'

The woman smiled, relieved, and moved on.

That was how it happened now. No explanations required.

By mid-afternoon, the library had settled into its quieter hours. Maggie took the opportunity to pull a box from the storage cupboard at the back—Arthur's notes, now catalogued and cleared for return. Harris had asked whether she wanted them archived or destroyed.

She'd chosen neither.

Instead, she'd sorted through them herself,

carefully, one step at a time. Not searching for meaning, just ensuring nothing important was lost. Most of the pages were observations. Dates. Cross-references. Questions he'd written for himself rather than anyone else. The slow work of someone who trusted process more than instinct.

She placed the box beneath the desk, out of sight but not forgotten.

That evening, Martin was waiting when she got home.

Not waiting, as in pacing or watching the road, just present, already there, the way he often was. He stood at the bench chopping vegetables, his movements steady, unhurried.

'You're late,' he said, without accusation.

'Lost track of time,' Maggie replied, setting her bag down. 'It happens again, apparently.'

He smiled faintly. 'Good sign.'

They cooked together without talking much, passing ingredients, adjusting heat, sharing the space with the ease that came from years of quiet understanding. When dinner was ready, they ate at the table by the window, the late light slipping across the floorboards.

Afterwards, Maggie cleared the plates while Martin made a pot of tea.

'You all right?' he asked, handing her a mug.

'Yes,' she said. Then, after a moment, 'Better than all right.'

He didn't press her to explain. Instead, they sat together, watching the day fade.

Later, Maggie returned to the jigsaw puzzle on the dining table. It had taken her longer than usual to finish this one. Not because it was difficult, but because she'd stopped rushing toward completion. She placed each piece deliberately, enjoying the small certainty of fit, the quiet satisfaction when something finally settled.

Martin leaned against the doorway, watching her work.

'You're nearly done,' he said.

'Mm.'

'You always slow down at the end.'

She smiled. 'It's the best part.'

When the final piece clicked into place, she didn't immediately move. She sat back slightly, looking at the whole picture. Not perfect. A corner slightly faded. One edge imperfectly cut.

Complete enough.

The next morning, Maggie walked the long way to work.

She didn't often take the river path anymore, not out of avoidance but out of choice. Today, though, she found herself turning toward it without conscious thought.

The path was dry, the water low and unremarkable. Sunlight caught on the surface in dull flashes.

She stopped at the spot where Arthur had been found.

Not because she felt compelled to, but because it felt appropriate.

There was no marker. No sign. Just the river, moving as it always had. Maggie stood there for a while, hands in her pockets, breathing evenly. She didn't think of the violence. She thought of Arthur at his desk, pencil in hand, making notes only he understood.

'He would have liked this,' she said quietly.

That was fine.

Life moved on in practical ways.

The council building reopened under new management. Committees were dissolved, reformed, restructured. There were audits. Reviews. Quiet resignations. Maggie observed it all from a distance, uninterested in the theatre of consequence. What mattered was that the mechanisms had been corrected. That the records were clean.

She was asked once whether she'd consider a formal advisory role.

She declined.

The library needed her more.

One afternoon, a young man approached her desk, nervous, earnest. He held a folder under his arm, knuckles white.

'I'm looking for land records,' he said. 'Historical ones.'

Maggie smiled, not unkindly. 'Tell me what you're looking for.'

As she guided him toward the correct shelves, she felt the satisfaction of continuity. This was how things should work. Questions asked. Answers sought. Systems functioning as intended.

That evening, she and Martin walked together along the main street, stopping briefly at the bakery, exchanging greetings with familiar faces. Nothing felt strained. Nothing needed explanation.

At home, Maggie opened Arthur's box again.

This time, she selected a single notebook and placed it on the shelf behind her desk. Not prominently. Just there.

A reminder, not a shrine.

Weeks later, on a day that felt no different from any other, Maggie realised she hadn't thought about the case at all.

The realisation startled her.

Then she let it go.

The river continued its work, shaping banks and carrying debris, indifferent to the stories imposed upon it. The library remained steady. Martin remained beside her, solid and present.

And Maggie, at last, allowed herself to be simply what she had always been.

A librarian.

A watcher.

Someone who noticed.

THE END

About the Author

Janene Morgan has loved stories for as long as she can remember and has dreamed of becoming an author since she was a young child. After years of writing courses, notebooks filled with ideas, and experimenting across different genres—from romance to children's stories and picture books — she finally found her stride writing cosy mysteries.

Secrets of the River is Janene's debut novel.

When she isn't writing, Janene can usually be found reading, baking, creating art, or travelling around Australia in a caravan with her family, always with a good book close by.

You can find Janene online at www.readsontheroad.com.au or on Instagram @reads_on_the_road